NEVER AS GOOD

AS THE FIRST

TIME

NEVER AS GOOD AS THE FIRST TIME

A novel

Jonathan Michael Hicks

Studio PUBLISHING

www.studiopub.com

Published by The Studio

Library of Congress Cataloging in Publication data available

10 9 8 7 6 5 3

LOOK FOR THESE FUTURE PROJECTS BY

"THE STUDIO"

Studio

SP

Publishing

BUTT NAKED, my soul exposed! (A NOVEL)

LOVE LETTERS ON THE WALL (A NOVEL)

BNAKED NEWSLETTER (JOIN NOW, LOG ON TO OUR WEBSITE)

MUSIC AND FILM RELEASES (GOING TO BE HOT! STAY TUNED)

A DEDICATION TO THE ARTS TOUR FEATURING POETS, AUTHORS, FILM DIRECTORS, MUSICANS AND MORE. (COMING TO A CITY NEAR YOU.)

A C K N O W L E D G M E N T S

There are many things I could say at this time. However, I've found through my maturity as a man and a writer, words are sometimes divine inspirations and must be chosen carefully.

With that sprinkle of love shared with you, I sit in prayer for the moment my spirit is inspired.

This is a love story for anyone who has gotten a second chance to love someone again.

P R O L O G U E

As a thirty-one year old paper-sack brown African American man, Jake Alexander was a handsome charmer. He stood with a muscular six foot two inch frame, had good hair that was short dark and curly, hazel eyes and a drop-dead smile with conversation to match. For him life with the opposite sex had always been a complicated easy.

In high school, Jake was much like all the other love-struck boys, who blushed at the very thought of a girl having a crush on them. That didn't mean he wasn't still quite the little ladies' man even as a teenager. Although he was shy, Jake still managed to keep plenty of girlfriends. Then in college things changed quite a bit. Jake had a different attitude and approach to his relationships with women. Mom's lessons about how he should treat them were long forgotten during his second semester at a small south Texas college when he pledged one of the black fraternities on the "yard." That's when his male superego kicked in and ran amuck. He was a big "frat man" now!

Jake knew fraternities provided a strong sense of unity for most of the brothers who joined them. Others simply wanted to use the fraternity like a pimp. They pimped the frat for the popularity it brought and for the women they thought they could get. Jake fell victim to the latter. He let his ego get fed to the point that he no longer had a sense of respect for other folks' feelings, especially women. It became all about lovin'em, then leavin'em!

His life of playing women as if they had become the latest hobby lasted for a little more than a year. Then Jake met Indigo Stuart. Oh, what a woman! She was born in Virginia and was one of the most beautiful and intelligent women on the campus. Indigo's pretty, soft, golden-brown skin was absolutely blemishless. She always worked-out at least twice a day, three times a week, and it showed in her shapely body. Indigo's legs were bowed and her calf muscles showed definition when she walked. Her waist was small and she sported her flat stomach by wearing midriff shirts every chance she got. Indigo's East Coast accent was noticeable in her sexy voice as she articulated words. When she talked, words flowed off her lips as if they were petals falling from a rose.

♥

Jake saw Indigo for the first time one day coming from class on the way to the gym. When he laid eyes on her, it was love at first sight! He followed her around campus for a whole week until finally he made his move and stopped Indigo on the way to the Laundromat. He asked if he could help carry her basket inside. She politely said "no", and insisted that he not ask again.

Despite the rejection, Jake still wanted Indigo's attention badly, and it became very obvious he wasn't going to let her leave without giving him some *play*. Keith Sweat would have been proud at the way Jake begged Indigo to go out with him. After she washed her clothes, Indigo finally agreed to have lunch with Jake, if for no other reason than to shut him up.

The next afternoon, Indigo and Jake met as agreed. Jake began their date by first apologizing for his persistent behavior at the Laundromat. Indigo gracefully accepted and suggested they move on with lunch because she had a full schedule of classes to attend.

During lunch, Jake and Indigo hit it off as if grade school sweethearts. Afterwards, they found themselves walking and talking for hours. Indigo even decided to miss her classes, which for the moment seemed unimportant.

Jake and Indigo's intense love affair went on for weeks, then months as their relationship continued through the spring semester. Just before the summer vacation started, Indigo decided to stay in town to accept an internship with a local advertising office. Jake however, needed to return home to Chicago to help his dad take care of his mother, who had surgery while Jake was taking his final exams.

As much as they hated to admit it, Indigo and Jake thought it would be best to take a break from each other to refocus their attention on school. Both their grades had suffered badly. Despite, the poor grades and the whirlwind affair, Jake and Indigo did know one thing; for the first time, they felt what real love was and this time, Jake thought, *"there would be no more broken hearts."*

♥

Once back in Chicago, Jake found his mother doing much better, and didn't need much help after all. His father seemed to have everything under control, leaving Jake with plenty of time to spend his days lying around thinking about Indigo. Then one day while he did his usual routine of daydreaming, the phone rang, and the big news hit!

"It sounds like something is wrong, Indigo!" asked Jake"

"I had to go to the doctor today."

"For what? Why didn't you say something about it earlier?"

"I'm saying something about it now. I'm pregnant!" The phone was silent as Indigo repeated, "Yes, I'm pregnant. Eleven weeks to be exact!"

Jake and Indigo now faced the biggest decision of their young lives. Neither was working full-time. Indigo's advertising job was only a part-time position and Jake wasn't employed at all. He had decided against taking a job to be available just in case things for his mother took a turn for the worse—at least, that was the bull-crap he kept telling himself. Now, with the possibility of he and Indigo becoming parents, Jake panicked and he found himself begging Indigo to consider getting an abortion, which only made matters worse and upset Indigo more.

Soon, Jake felt tremendously guilty for asking Indigo to consider killing the life of their child. He realized if Indigo had an abortion, she would not only be killing the baby, but a part of her would die too!

After a deep breath, Jake reassured Indigo they were in this together and apologized for ever suggesting she kill their baby. Then he comforted her by assuring her everything would be all right and promised no matter what, he was going to be by her side.

"There are some sorry-ass Negroes out there who have fathered children and don't give a damn about taking care of them. But not me!" assured Jake.

Hearing Jake talk like a real man, and not like a little boy trying to run from trouble, made Indigo feel much better. She now was eager to hear how they were going to handle things from here on out. After all, they both were still full-time students and had bright futures ahead of them.

Indigo however, was also very afraid that she wasn't going to finish school. She only had one year and a half to go, but now it looked like she would have to quit for a while and find a full-time job. The trailer she lived in was a matchbox and no place to raise a child. Jake would have to finally get off his ass and find a job back in Texas next semester. In fact Indigo thought, he had better start looking harder for a permanent position to take as soon as he graduated in the summer.

Jake and Indigo stayed on the phone, eagerly discussing plans for the unborn child's life. After they hung up, Jake realized time was getting short and his summer fun in the sun was over. He had a family to look after now. "Yeah, I'm going to be a parent, a father, a daddy!" said Jake proudly.

There were also other things to think about, like what Indigo's mother was going to think about her being pregnant, especially by a man with no job! Oh, and Jake's mother would probably have two heart attacks and be ready to kick somebody's ass! She always told Jake that he'd better not come home with anything he didn't leave with. Most definitely, no babies!

His mother had been married to his father for forty-five years and was old-fashioned in her views about one-parent families. She disapproved of them wholeheartedly. However, Indigo's situation was totally different. Her father had left her mother when she was only five years old. To make ends meet, her mother worked two jobs, while trying to raise Indigo and her two younger brothers. As far as Indigo's mother was concerned, men weren't worth a damn and who needed 'em!

Pamela Julia Johnson and Kayra Austin were both from Houston, Texas. They had been friends since the fifth grade. And even then, Pam would always get Kayra in and out of trouble.

Nevertheless, Kayra and Pam's relationship continued to grow over the years despite Kayra's parents limiting the time they spent together—an effort to minimize Pam's bad influence. But once they graduated from high school, each decided to go their separate ways in life. By the late fall season, Pam went to college out west in California; Kayra remained in Texas.

After two long years of failing grades and near academic probation, Pam decided she needed more excitement in her life. She wanted a career where she could put her outgoing personality to use. Through the contacts she made in California, she was introduced to a public relations agent or publicist as they're known in the "biz", who represented several big name Hollywood celebrities. He suggested Pam consider a career in public relations. Two months later she withdrew from school.

After several small assignments with local Los Angeles radio and television stations, Pam discovered having contacts in a town like Los Angeles didn't mean shit, unless you were fucking somebody; which wasn't a problem, except there were already plenty of aspiring "whatevers" doing that. So Pam decided to leave Los Angeles for Chicago. At least in the *Windy City* she could make a fresh start. Luckily, not long after she got there, Pam met a charming older man who loved the way she made him feel. After many weeks of screwing his brains out, she was able to talk him into giving her enough money to open her own public relations agency in Chicago. Hey, it's the American way!

Kayra stayed in Texas and completed her degree in education. After a few years of working dead-end jobs, she finally was able to put away a nice savings and decided it was time to make a change. So, she called Pam to ask her what the job market was like in Chicago. Of course, Pam didn't even bother to check.

The next week Pam called Kayra and lied to her about all of the fantastic job opportunities she checked on for her. She suggested Kayra come stay with her for a while until she got settled. Kayra's move to Chicago would no doubt also be to her advantage.

Although she was an attractive woman, Pam knew Kayra always ate healthy and worked out faithfully. Pam prayed Kayra would help her get rid of those extra pounds she had packed onto her five-foot seven inch frame since they had last seen each other. For some strange reason, Pam could not find another friend who was willing to put up with her big mouth. Besides, it would be nice to have her best friend around. Despite all the shit Pam had put Kayra through over the years, Kayra always stuck by Pam no matter what.

Growing up, Kayra was quiet and soft-spoken, unlike Pam who always wanted attention. Kayra never desired to be a part of the "in crowd." Now as far as she was concerned, Chicago was going to be her real coming-out party. With the help of Pam, Kayra thought she was going to start a new life despite Pam's history of getting her into shit that was easy to get into but hard to get out of. Kayra wondered if the invitation from Pam to come to the *Windy City* was another one of those times again, but she convinced herself she had a lot to gain no matter what Pam had up her sleeve.

Two weeks after talking to Pam, Kayra loaded up her 1981 Pacer she had since the 12th grade. "That's okay!" she thought. It wouldn't be long before she would keep her promise to herself and buy a new BMW M3 for her 30th birthday next year. Kayra settled on the reality that she would be stuck riding a "hoopty" for a while, until she got on her feet in Chicago.

♥

When Sunday morning came. Kayra kissed her family good-bye and headed northeast to Chicago. She reached the city three days, two speeding tickets, and one flat tire later. Once she was in town, she stopped at a gas station and called Pam, who had been pacing the floor for the past four hours waiting to hear from her. As Kayra waited for Pam to come meet her, she thought, "*At last I have what I've been looking forward to for so long -- a chance to get away from Texas and make it on my own.*"

THAT WAS THEN. THIS IS NOW...

Chapter 1

*I*t seemed like it had been a lifetime ago since Jake and Indigo were married, finished school and then later divorced. The failed relationship crushed both of them. Jake blamed himself for not being the husband he should have been. And Indigo believed somehow she could had done more to keep her and Jake together. Nothing short of a miracle kept Jake and Indigo in college while also trying to raise their small child, Railey. They both had stayed in school an extra year to meet all of the graduation requirements. But under the circumstances, it seemed like a small price to pay to be able to properly take care of their beautiful son.

By the time Indigo graduated, Jake had already started his career in retail, having finished school earlier that year. But then the stress of parenting, working and marriage soon became too much for the young couple. Indigo divorced Jake, took Railey, and moved to New York to begin her career in advertising. Jake left for Chicago to work as a manager for a major retail chain, in hopes of one day owning his own men's store.

♥

Now a few short years after the divorce, the new love of Jake's life was Kayra, whom he met this year just after the Christmas holiday. It was on a casual afternoon when both Kayra and Jake were at the mall. Kayra was volunteering her time there to sign-up more African Americans to be bone marrow donors for a local hospital. While, Jake was scouting the competition of his men's clothing store.

In many ways, Kayra reminded Jake of Indigo. Nevertheless, this was the beginning of a wonderful four-month courtship. They spent every moment together and made passionate love every chance they got, which was definitely a change for Kayra, who before Jake, was not very sexually active at all. Mainly, because when she did, Kayra felt more like she was being fucked instead of being made love too. Not with Jake. When she was with him, Kayra never felt such tenderness from a man before.

But in the back of both their minds, Jake and Kayra kept reminding themselves of their history of falling head-over-heels in love, later to find *themselves, by themselves*

♥

Their love affair was kept on the "down low" from each of their close friends, Malik and Pam. They knew once those two found out, they would have to listen to a bunch of shit from them.

Now the time had come for Jake and Kayra to let the truth be known, as it became harder and harder for them to keep up the game of pretending not to be in love. Today was the big day to break the big news to them.

Jake went to Malik's apartment to tell him about his relationship with Kayra.

"Man, I don't know how to say this other than to come straight out with it. I've met this beautiful

16

woman who's got it going on! Her name is Kayra -- Kayra Austin. We've been seeing each other for the past four months, and I think I'm in love with her!"

Jake sat back and began to briefly tell Malik about how his first date with Kayra had ended.

"Jake, I had a wonderful time tonight."

"Well then, can I walk you inside?"

"No, we better just say good night. I have to get up early in the morning and run some errands."

"I understand Kayra. The last thing I want to do is seem too pushy."

Jake looked into Kayra's eyes and moved his sexy full lips closer to hers.

"I don't kiss on the first date," Kayra said quickly. She paused. "But be sure to try on the second!"

Kayra smiled and walked up the stairs to her apartment. Jake watched and admired her smooth shapely legs holding up her hourglass figure. Smiling, he realized even with a petite body, she still had a plump ass, which looked like a beating heart as she glided up the stairs.

"Yeah baby!" shouted Jake.

Malik interrupted, "You mean to tell me you've been hiding this for four months! Man, I've known you ever since we were little boys playing hide and go seek. It seems like you've been in love a million times. It's kinda funny, you have always had this dream lover in your head. I guess you think of this one as 'Mrs. Right,' too and that you're going to ride off into some big-ass sunset and live happily ever after. But I know what's going to happen. You're gonna' end up getting hurt. In fact, you've had so many 'Mrs. Wrong's' you shouldn't want 'Mrs. Right!' It's okay to dream, Jake, but I don't want to see you get hurt again. Besides, my brother, you need to find a sister to date, instead of always getting with those white girls all the time!"

"Look Malik! My girl Kayra is a sista'," said Jake angrily as he stood up from the table. "I don't feel like hearing one of your pro-black speeches today! It wasn't that long ago before you got into this, 'I'm black and I'm proud shit', that your name was just Ricky before you ran off and changed it to Malik. And if I'm not mistaken, you were trying to get all the white pussy you could find. As a matter of fact, I remember the girl in the 12th grade who you were so proud of."

"What girl?" asked Malik.

"You know the one. She had mangy red hair and a big zit on her nose. You thought you were *all that, plus tax* when you were walking around holding hands with her."

"Man quit lying!" shouted Malik.

"Oh, my brother, you want to forget those days," said Jake.

"I don't want to forget anything!" answered Malik. "I ain't in the 12th grade anymore. I am a twenty-seven year-old black man who refuses to be enslaved by the white hypocrisy and subtle manipulation to keep us as nothing but niggers!"

"No, your ass need a job! All your broke ass want to do is sit around talking that whitie shit. Take your ass and get a job Negro! I'm sorry, Ricky -- oh, I mean Malik."

Although he didn't want to admit it, Jake knew Malik was right about him falling in love so much. When they were young kids in high school, Jake had sweetheart after sweetheart. He would bring different girls home to meet his mother and confess his love for them. Two weeks later, he would forget about each of them and be on his new love. Jake's mother tried to tell him it was not necessary, nor was it her desire to play mother-in-law each week. Her point was; don't bring every girl you meet home to your mother. *The mother introduction is to be saved for the special someone with whom you have a real relationship with.*

♥

Jake felt bad about how hard he was on Malik. He had always been there for him. So to try and make up with him, Jake decided he would call Malik and ask if he wanted to go out to a new night club to talk and have a couple of drinks.

"Hello."

"What's up man? This is Jake."

"What do you want?"

Jake felt the coldness in Malik's voice and tried to explain. "Look man I wanted to apologize for the way I acted earlier. I shouldn't have played you like that because I know that you are just concerned about me. We're like brothers and there's no reason for us to try to hurt each other."

Malik thought about it for a moment, then told Jake, "Sometimes family just can't get along!"

"But we've been through too much together to just say fuck it!" replied Jake. "I tell you what, I was thinking about going to that new club on 22nd Street. I think the name of it is *Jasmine.* Anyway, they say it's pretty hot with plenty of hoochees!"

"What about that girl you told me about? You know she's got your nose wide open. Aren't you supposed to get with her tonight?"

"Yeah, but I decided to give that a break for tonight. I'm going to take your advice and move slow on this one."

"I'm glad. What time are we heading out?"

"Well, I like to get there early and leave late!" answered Jake. "I say, let's roll about 9:30pm. Be ready!"

Jake hung up the phone and thought about what he was going to tell Kayra. He remembered mentioning they would do something together tonight. He was afraid if he canceled she would ask a lot of questions and he didn't want to lie. After pacing the floor for about an hour, Jake got up the nerve to call.

"Hi, Kayra."

"Hello, Jake."

"How's my brown queen?"

"I'm fine, just a little nervous about talking to Pam today. I've haven't got up the nerve to tell her yet, but I will in a few minutes, I promise."

"Don't worry, it'll be okay. Let me tell you about how Malik took it about us."

"Oh yeah! What did he say?"

"Baby he was trippin' at first. We got into this big argument and I ended saying some things that I think hurt his feelings. But I think he's going to be okay about us once a little time goes by. I did apologize and hmmm, I also ---"

"That's good, I know everything is going to be alright," interrupted Kayra. "We'll all be sitting around having dinner in a couple weeks, laughing about this whole thing. I guess I had better go tell Pam. Oh, I almost forgot, did you decide where we're going tonight?"

Jake turned his head from the phone. "Damn!" he whispered. "That's what I wanted to talk to you about. After I apologized to Malik, I wanted to try and clear things up, so I invited him to go out with me for a drink or two."

Sounding very disappointed, Kayra told Jake that it was okay and that she understood. She also told him that she appreciated his honesty. Jake asked Kayra to forgive him for backing out of their date, and promised to make it up to her.

♥

Kayra went to Pam's house disappointed about not being able to be with Jake, but she was still excited about finally telling Pam all about her steamy relationship with him.

"Pam, you never asked me what I did during the Christmas holidays or why I've been acting kinda strange lately."

"Well shit, Kayra! After the way you acted when I did try asking what was up with you, I figured you didn't want me in your business."

"I guess you're right, but girl let me tell you anyway! I've been waiting four long months to let you in on the scoop because I wanted to be sure about the brother first. You remember that so-called "chocolate drop" you said you saw me with a few months ago."

Pam's eyes lit up.

"Yes I remember, *mister ass and chest.*"

"Okay, Pam!"

"Alright I'll stop, just tell me what happened."

20

Kayra continued with the details. "His name is Jake. Jake Alexander. That's who I've been seeing since September. I can still remember our first date. Jake called me while I was soaking in the tub." Kayra closed her eyes and thought back to the unforgettable day when Jake made his first call to her. "Hmmm, I can hear him now."

"Hi. This is Jake Alexander, the guy you met at the mall last week."

"Yes, I remember you. Didn't we exchange phone numbers?"

"Well, Kayra, yes we did. Why didn't you call me? What's the problem, you're not interested in me anymore?"

Kayra thought for a moment. Then she answered. "I haven't made up my mind one way or another about you. I'm not sure if I am interested in you or not."

Kayra hoped Jake wasn't turned off by her playing hard-to-get. The truth of the matter was, she had been crazy about him from the moment they met. But this time caution was key. Kayra was determined not to be disappointed like she had been many times before by "low-budget" brothers who were only out to get their groove on. For some reason though, Jake made her feel different and before she knew it she had let down her guard long enough to give him her phone number.

"Well, Kayra if that's the case please allow me to invite you to dinner, I think that might help us get to know one another better. I believe you will be very pleased if you do."

"Jake, I don't know if that's a good idea."

"Look Kayra, you are a gorgeous woman. After I talked to you the day we met, I discovered that your outside beauty is just a reflection of the beauty that is on the inside of you. And if nothing else, I need another chance to see that lovely smile of yours to warm my soul and brighten my day."

Kayra began to blush and finally, she decided it was time to lose the "hard-to-get" routine and get with this fine brown sugar of a man.

"Alright! Yes Jake, I will have dinner with you. When would you like to go?"

Jake quickly answered, "How about eight o'clock?"

"Do you mean tonight?" asked Kayra, surprised by Jake's invitation.

"Yes tonight. I'll be there at eight o'clock sharp! Oh, and by the way, don't worry about giving me your address. I do my homework."

Kayra smiled and whispered to herself, "No he didn't insist on me going." She thought about it, "I like the take-charge kind of man. Okay, Jake, you win! I'll see you at eight o'clock."

"Pam, after that, I hung up the phone and leaped out the tub so fast I almost broke my damn neck!"

Before Kayra could get to the rest of the details, Pam asked, "Did you get some?"

"Some of what?" Kayra asked.

"You know what I'm talking about! Let me put it this way. Did you get some sex, do the wild thing, bump and grind?"

"No Pam, we didn't—just a kiss."

Pam kept her cool and walked away shaking her head.

"I'll leave that alone!" she said quietly.

Chapter 2

Kayra went home and thanked God it was Friday. Pam, was her usual very restless self checking her closet for the leather dresses she had bought when she and Kayra went shopping a few weeks earlier. "Yeah, this is the one!" She pulled out the sexy red dress with the low-cut neckline. It showed so much cleavage, it hardly left anything to the imagination and sported a split that went damn near up to her hipbone. Pam quickly went to slip it on. She looked in the mirror and modeled for herself by making turns and posing. Finally, she stopped and took a long look at her reflection and thought how all that hard work in the gym had paid off. For a while there, she was overweight and couldn't buy the attention of a man. She looked so unattractive, or at least she felt that way. Now her shapely body and toned muscles made her the sparkle of men's eyes.

These days, she was the new and improved Pamela Julia Johnson, who is in control of her life.

"Damn, I'm just too fine!" she shouted as

24

she turned and walked away from the mirror laughing. "So it's settled," she yelled taking off the leather dress and heading straight for the phone to call Kayra to see what her plans were for the night.

While the phone rang Pam thought, "I bet Kayra is out with Mr. A.C. (ass & chest). Kayra answered.

"Girl, Jake canceled our date because of a fight with his friend, Malik."

"What that got to do with you? Does he always let problems with his friends keep him from his woman?"

"Don't even try going there, Pam. Jake is a good brother. This is the first time something like this has ever happened, which by the way was after he told Malik about us. That's why Jake and I had decided to wait a while before telling you and Malik that we are in love."

"Not the old, *I'm in love again*, shit!"

"See that's probably how Jake's friend reacted and how they got into an argument. Anyway, Jake apologized and invited him for a drink so they could talk. That's that!"

"Sounds weak to me! But I'm glad you're free for the night." To lighten things up, Pam suggested they go out to the new club in town and do some partying. Kayra agreed it would be nice to go somewhere different.

"*Jasmine* it is then," replied Kayra.

♥

By eight o'clock Jake was getting ready for his night out on the town with Malik. "I got an hour to get dressed and pick him up. Now, what should I throw on tonight?"

Jake's success as the owner of two top-selling men's clothing stores proved to have its benefits. He was one of the best-dressed men in Chicago. "I'll just put on a little sumthin', sumthin'!" crooned Jake, while looking through his tailor-made suits in just about every color to fit his discriminating taste. When he wore one, he knew he looked good! The suits were cut to show his broad shoulders, while still flowing down the rest of his tall muscular body. When he walked, he was poetry in

25

motion. Every woman who saw him couldn't help but admire his presence.

Malik was not quite as polished, and needed the fashion patrol called on his ass for some of the shit he tried to wear. He stood looking into his small unorganized closet, wondering what to wear to keep Jake from making fun of him.

Meanwhile, Jake thought since things were kinda uneasy between him and Malik, he wasn't going to start shit with him about what he wore. "Whatever my boy steps out in tonight is cool with me. Even if he looks straight out of the Brady Bunch, I'm not going to say a word about it!"

Jake chose to wear wide-leg, cuffed gray slacks with a caramel cashmere blazer, a hand-made gray and caramel vest, and a fresh white French-cut shirt. Just to add a little flavor, he pulled out a pair of camel, eel-skinned shoes. Afterwards, he took a relaxing bath in his whirlpool tub and groomed his jet-black hair then sculpted his outfit piece by piece like a fine craftsman, until the product was finished. He looked in the mirror and stopped to think how badly he wished Kayra could see how good he looked. "If she could see me now, she would fall into my arms and be mine forever! Maybe I should call her to see if she wants to go with us tonight. No." Jake thought, he couldn't do that to Malik. They were already on shaky grounds and a move like that might be all they needed to end their friendship. Instead, the idea came to him to stop by Kayra's house on his way to pick up Malik; he still could keep his date with him and give Kayra the chance to see him. Just before he got to Kayra's house, Jake stopped at a late-night florist shop and bought a beautiful, long-stemmed rose. "Can't go there empty-handed," said Jake.

♥

Outside Kayra's house, Jake was surprised to find all the lights on and the music turned up loud, bumping Maxwell's new jam "Ascension." Instead of going to the door and knocking, Jake went around to the back. He noticed Kayra's bedroom light on and peeked through the window. He saw Kayra standing in the mirror fixing herself while singing and bopping her head to the music. He also observed that Kayra didn't look too broken up by their canceled date. In fact, she acted like it hadn't affected her at all. "I thought she would be sitting around doing nothing," mumbled Jake as he admired how wonderful she looked. "Where does she think she's going?"

He didn't know whether he should go back around to the front and ring the doorbell, or go quietly without saying anything. At this point he thought it would be best just to leave well enough alone and go pick up Malik.

♥

Jake got to Malik's apartment and pulled in the driveway. He looked down at the rose he was going to give to Kayra, picked it up and thought it was too pretty to throw away. "I might as well not waste it." He took it with him to Malik's door and knocked. When Malik opened the door, he reached and gave him the rose and said, "Here you go sweetheart. Now give daddy a big kiss!"

Malik snatched the rose from Jake and the two of them burst out laughing. Jake went inside the apartment and waited for Malik to make some last-minute adjustments with his gear for the night, and as he did, Jake checked out what Malik had on. Just as he thought, Malik had on a whacked outfit. He wore a pair of tan wool pants with a tight brown turtleneck sweater. To top it all off, he sported a shit brown, pleather, three-quarter-length coat. Jake kept his promise and was determined not to say a word. He did decide, however, he was going to try one more time to get Malik into his store to help him with a new hip look. Unfortunately, it couldn't be tonight!

♥

It was time for Pam to go pick up Kayra, but before she went out the door, Pam took one final look in the mirror to glance at her seductive leather dress. She also adjusted her breasts so they would be in the right position to look "suckable." Her short black fingerwaved hair with a hint of platinum at the ends looked healthy and shiny.

After making sure everything was just right, she grabbed her purse and headed for the door. She wondered if tonight was the right time to talk to Kayra about something she had had on her mind for a long time. "No," she thought, "I'll save it for another time. Tonight is not the night."

When she got to her car, she had to ease herself inside because the dress was too tight and she could barely move, even though she looked like a page from a Hollywood magazine. The next problem, Pam was seriously broke tonight. It was the first of the month and she had a lot of bills to pay, after all she was an independent woman with her own business. That was more than allot of brothers she knew could say. And in opinion it didn't matter if all she had in her purse was twenty dollars. She knew she looked good—broke or not! Twenty dollars would be enough to get her in the club. The rest would be up to the dress and a little charm. "Men are suckers for a pretty face and a big ass!" she said laughing.

Chapter 3

*J*ake and Malik arrived at the club at 9:30pm just as they had planned. It was still very early and the club wasn't jumpin' yet. The crowd was small with a steady flow of people coming in.

It was Jake and Malik's first time at *Jasmine*. They looked around checking things out like two tourists. Who could blame them? The club was magnificent! The furniture and doors were royal burgundy with every rail, handle, and knob trimmed in gold. Each chair and couch was made of soft leather that hugged you when you sat on them.

On the walls were hand painted originals by black artists such as Annie Lee, Ernie Barnes, Ernest Watson and John Farrar. Sculptures by Leroy Jackson filled the lobby.

Jake seemed to be the most impressed with the sunken lounge in the center of the club. It was surrounded by soundproof, smoked glass, which kept the outside noise out and the smooth jazz in. For those who wanted to get their romance on, a fireplace aided the private and cozy atmosphere.

♥

Pam arrived at Kayra's house and rang the doorbell five times but Kayra still didn't answer. Pam heard the music playing, so she thought it would be a good idea if she went around back and knocked on the window. She knew how Kayra was; she was the only woman she knew that didn't have a man, but spent most of the time in the mirror. Pam banged on the bedroom window. Sure enough, there was Kayra getting all "dolled up".

The sound of the window shaking startled Kayra. She dropped the brush and turned around with eyes the size of half-dollars. Pam laughed, then pointed her finger at the door for Kayra to open it. When she let her in, Pam quickly apologized and so did Kayra for not being ready.

"All I have to do is put on some lipstick, then I'll be ready." Instead of answering, Pam couldn't take her eyes off Kayra. She marveled at how lovely she looked and followed her to the restroom. Pam stood in the doorway staring as Kayra put on lipstick. Kayra's long, jet-black hair was always down, and it laid on her shoulders like a curtain of silk. The form-fitting black dress grazed her body ever so slightly, just enough for her figure to show without being too tight. To add a touch of class, she wore a pearl choker. She was gorgeous!

♥

Pam and Kayra finally got out of the house and started on their way to the club.

"Did you get a chance to talk to Jake again?" asked Pam.

"No, I didn't bother trying to call him."

Pam frowned and stopped talking. After a moment of a very uncomfortable silence, Pam asked, "What is it that you like so much about him? I mean, I know he's fine and all that, but what is he about?"

"Well, he's gentle and kind. He is also very attentive and interested in me without making me feel like an object he's after. I don't know, it's just something about him. He just seems different that's all! Why? Do you think something is wrong? You seem to be upset."

"It's okay. Nothing's wrong." Pam replied. But the look on her face told a different story.

"Is there something on your mind?" asked Kayra.

"No, I said!" yelled Pam "I just wanted to know what was up between you and him. I mean, I've been your girl for a long time and I know I've gotten you in plenty of shit, but things have changed. We're women now, and I don't want to push you into doing something that you will regret later. In other words, I just care about you!"

"Pam don't feel like you're pushing me to do anything. You're right, we're not little girls anymore, and frankly, I decided a long time ago that I wasn't going to let you pull the wool over my eyes again." The two laughed and hugged. Then the car swerved.

"Okay, we'd better stop this before you kill us both!" laughed Kayra.

Pam turned, looked Kayra in the eyes, and held her hand. "I really do care about you Kayra. Are you ready to paint the town tonight? You think you can hang with me?"

"Pam, I can hang with you anytime and anyplace!"

"Girl, please!" replied Pam. "Well, we're just about there. Look, there it is! Seems like it is getting pretty crowded. Oh, check out the fellows!" Pam rolled down her window and yelled, "Black men, black men, I love ya!"

Kayra slid down in the seat and covered her face with embarrassment. "Cut it out, Pam!"

"I told you, you won't be able to hang with me tonight. Anyway don't worry, I'm just having a little fun, Kayra. I won't get us into any trouble. I promise."

"I'll be watching you, Pam."

32

♥

Jake and Malik sat at the bar and ordered two beers. Malik noticed two nice looking women checking him and Jake out. He leaned over to Jake and whispered, "Hey Jake, you see those two honeys over there?"

"Where?" asked Jake.

"Don't look now." Malik rolled his eyes over to the left to let Jake know where to look. As soon as he did, Jake turned around immediately.

"I thought I told you not to look now!" said Malik angrily.

Jake turned back around to Malik. "Sorry about that." After a few minutes passed, Jake turned again and this time he tried not to look obvious.

"You see the one in the white dress?" asked Malik. Before Jake could answer, Malik said, "See, she's looking over here smiling again?" Malik stopped talking to Jake and focused his attention on the woman. He smiled back and gestured a toast to her with his glass. She returned the toast and signaled Malik to come over to her table.

"I told you." said Malik excitedly.

"She does look good!" replied Jake. "Is that her friend sitting next to her?"

"I don't know, but I'll find out what's up for you," answered Malik.

Jake pushed Malik. "Go on, throw that rap on 'em! Whatcha waitin' on?"

"Nothing!" answered Malik.

"Well, if you don't go, I will!" replied Jake.

"Alright!" said Malik, "here goes nothing."

Malik got up and nervously walked to the other side of the bar. He smiled, "Hi, how are you ladies doing tonight?"

"I'm doing fine," one of them answered.

Malik looked down and saw she wasn't wearing any panties. He caught himself staring with his mouth hanging wide open and tried to play it off. "Hi, I'm Malik. What is your name?"

"Nicole."

"You sure look good tonight," complimented Malik.

"Thank you," answered Nicole.

"What brings you out here tonight?" asked Malik.

Nicole turned to her friend sitting in the chair next to her. "This is my girlfriend, Yolanda. Yolanda, this is Malik."

"Hi," said Malik quietly.

"Hello, Malik."

"Yolanda and I weren't doing anything tonight, so we thought we would come see the show."

"What show?" asked Malik.

"The comedy show they have before the dancing starts. This must be your first time here," answered Nicole.

"Yes, as a matter of fact it is."

"Who's your friend?" asked Yolanda while smiling and licking her thick sexy lips.

"That's my partner Jake. He's the one who talked me into coming here tonight. It's his first time too!"

"Well, let me introduce him to Yolanda when we come back over here a little later," said Nicole eagerly. She smiled and with a very sexy voice said, "It was really nice meeting you, Malik."

"By the way," said Yolanda, "your friend over there is kinda cute."

"He sure is, girl," agreed Nicole, "but I think Malik here has got it going on too! I like the outfit you have on. Do you always dress so different?"

Malik regained his composure. "Yes, I do. I'll admit I'm a little weak in the fashion department, but at the same time, people shouldn't always be concerned with what's on the outside. We should focus on our African heritage and what it represents inside us."

"Go on my brother," joked Nicole. "Why don't you go get your friend while we go to the little girl's room for a moment."

"Cool," replied Malik.

Nicole winked, "We'll be right back."

When they left, Malik ran to where Jake was sitting. "It's about time man!" Jake replied. "I thought you forgot about me. While you were gone, this girl who looked like Wanda from *In Living Color* tried to get me to take her home. Anyway, what's up?"

"Man, those honeys are fine as hell!" I think that Nicole girl has the hots for me! They were talking like they wanted to get with us."

"They did? Shit, let's go before Wanda gets back! Where did they go?" asked Jake.

"Oh, they went to the restroom for a minute. They'll be right back," answered Malik.

"Did they say anything about me?" asked Jake, to see if he had gotten any play.

"They thought you were cute. But I cleared that up. I told them they should hold that thought until they got a chance to see you up close!"

Jake started laughing. "No, you didn't go there!"

"Hey, here they come now."

"Where?" asked Jake.

"Right here!"

"So who do we have here?" asked Yolanda.

"Jake, this is Nicole and Yolanda. Nicole and Yolanda, this Jake."

Jake gently kissed each of their hands. "Hello, ladies."

Yolanda began to shoot her rap at Jake. She looked him up and down with her large, sexy eyes. She stopped at the bulge she saw growing in his pants and smiled. "So Jake, what brings you out tonight?"

"Well, Malik and I had a little reconciling to do, so I figured what better way than to come out and relax. Who knows, maybe we'll get lucky and meet two beautiful women to sweep us off our feet."

Yolanda looked at Nicole. "He's charming too, girl!"

"What about you two? Where are you from?" asked Jake.

"Milwaukee. We work for the same company. We have tomorrow off and decided to come to Chicago for the night. Have some fun."

"You're staying the night?" asked Malik in disbelief, as if he just couldn't be that lucky.

"Yes. We have a suite at the Marriot on 54th street."

Malik grabbed Jake's knee under the bar to signal him to lay on the charm. They both were thinking the same thing. *"Booty Call!"*

"Let's have some fun then!" said Jake. He moved closer to Yolanda and whispered in her ear.

"You're the sexiest women I've ever seen." Yolanda giggled and thanked him for the compliment.

"Can I get you ladies something to drink?" asked Jake. He sensed he was making progress with Yolanda and signaled the bartender to come to the counter.

"Yes sir, may I help you?"

"Can you bring us a couple of bottles of Moet, please?" answered Jake.

"Yes, I'll be right back."

As soon as the bartender walked away, Yolanda promptly "got her peep on." She couldn't keep her eyes off Jake. She even moved closer to him and rested her thigh on his knee. Then she leaned into him so he could feel her breast on his arm.

Nicole was just as excited about Malik and all he could do was sit there and smile. "Malik, do you have a wife, girlfriend, or a significant other?" asked Nicole.

"No, to all of the above," answered Malik.

"Good!" she replied

Nicole was a native of a small South African township and had moved to the United States with her father when she was eleven. She had a real appreciation for Malik's views and his sense of heritage. "So what if he looked like a square," she thought. *"At least he was genuine and not one of those fake men trying to advertise all their financial assets. Many women miss golden opportunities to get to know a generous, genuine, and kind man. Instead, they flock to the knuckleheads.* thought Nicole, as she quickly realized Malik was a good catch!

Chapter 4

s Kayra and Pam drove up to the club, they saw the massive crowd hanging outside the front door.

"Why is everybody packed at the front?" asked Kayra.

"They're waiting to get picked to go inside," explained Pam.

"Picked?" asked Kayra.

"Yeah, they do it a lot in California too, sort of a Hollywood type thing. The door manager stands at the front door and looks for who he thinks is pretty enough, cool enough, or hip enough to go inside and enjoy the party. Crazy, huh?"

"It sure is!" replied Kayra. "Let's valet park tonight. Normally I think it's a waste of money, but what the hell!"

Pam cruised her 'Vette up to the front entry. Everyone who was standing around stopped talking and stared at the car to see if celebrities stepped out. The attendants opened the doors and Pam and Kayra slowly got out of the car. All eyes were on them! They were unquestionably the most gorgeous women there. They instantly became a hit with both men and women. In fact, the door manager was so impressed, he called them up to the front. He smiled and insisted Pam and Kayra come inside as his guests — free of charge. Of course, they gracefully accepted. As they entered, Pam looked back over her shoulder and whispered to Kayra, "I told you!"

♥

The large crowd inside made Kayra feel a little uncomfortable. "Pam, I don't know about this. There sure are a lot of people in here."

"Of course there are! Look at all our fans." Pam pointed to all the men who were glancing and staring at them. Even the men who were with someone tried to be slick by pretending they were looking for a waitress. That gave them just the opportunity they needed to turn around and check them out.

Afterwards, a waiter walked up to Kayra and Pam. "Excuse me, may I seat you ladies? The show will be starting in just a few minutes."

"What show?" asked Kayra.

Pam interrupted. "It's a comedy show. A comic comes on stage for about thirty minutes to get the crowd relaxed and going before the real party starts."

After explaining, Pam told the waiter, "Sure, we would like to be seated." He escorted them to their seats, which were only a few rows from the stage. "Here you are". He slid each chair back and made sure they were comfortable before he left.

♥

Jake, Malik, Nicole, and Yolanda were still at the bar getting relaxed with each other. They played a few drinking games, which became an excuse to touch and feel on one another. Both Jake and Yolanda took advantage of the time and made plans to make sex later—and were ready to go. They both had gotten horny after Yolanda tried to hold Jake's hand, which

39

happened to be in his lap at the time. As she did, he guided her hand to his bulge, and then she started rubbing it. One thing led to another and things got very freaky. Yolanda wanted to give him some head right there at the bar. Jake saw a couple of people checking all the action going on under the bar, so he chickened out.

Malik and Nicole were just beginning to get their own little show going when the stage lights popped on and the curtain drew back. "It must be time for the comic to come out," said Jake.

"Ladies and gentlemen, I would like to thank you for coming out to *Jasmine* tonight. As always, before we get the party started, we'd like to present you with a little comic entertainment. With no further adieu, here's *Special K*. He's the man who is here to drop you some knowledge as well as make you laugh. Ladies and gentlemen, *Special K*."

The audience gave a warm applause as the handsome comedian walked on stage with his gray, baggy designer suit, which was tailored to the tee!

"What's up Chicago! How's everybody doing tonight? Well, it's a pleasure being here in Jasmine, the hottest club in the 'Windy City.' We're gonna have some fun, but in order to do that, we've got to be honest with each other tonight. After all, isn't honesty the key to everything in life?" The crowd responded by giving a big round of applause. *"I mean, can we talk up in here like some real folk?"*

"Yeah!" shouted the audience.

"Okay, now raise your hand if you don't have a job."

Everybody got silent, as if they were too embarrassed to respond. Nobody raised their hand. *"I'm not trying to call you out or put nobody on the spot. I know most of you want to work but ain't found nothing yet, but you are looking! So this ain't for those of you sitting on their ass everyday smoking a joint conversating about the man is keeping you down. No. No. No. What I'm about say ain't for you people, but for the other people trying to do something about the struggle they're in. I want you to know that not working is nothing to be*

40

ashamed of, as long as you're trying to do something about it."

"I'm going to ask one more time. How many of you aint't got a job?" This time hands go up in the air without hesitation. *"Okay, that's better! Now those of you sitting next to somebody with their hand up, I want you to introduce yourself and tell them where you're working at. Then both of you exchange some basic personal information. Those of you who need a job, use that person you just met as a personal reference and go apply for a job at his or her company."*

"Now, men don't go up to the place and tell them folks, 'Yo, my man told me to come through and check you out about a gig.' Ladies you too! Don't you go and tell them, 'Girl, my other girl said you can hook a sister up with a J-O-B since I can't find a B.M.W. (black man working). You know how that is, don't you girl?'"

"We've got to take control of this shit and help pull one another up. Hook a nigger up!"

The club roared with applause and everybody stood in agreement. *"Alright! Sit your asses down! Now since we're being for real up in here, I got another question for you. How many of you are on food stamps?"* The audience got silent again and nobody raised a hand.

"Oh, so I'm the only one! I know you're lying. I was downtown today picking up my stamps and some of your asses look familiar!" The crowd burst out laughing. *"I'm just kidding, I'm not even trying to go there."*

"Hey, let's talk about sex. How many of you use protection each and every time you have sex?" All hands go up instantly. *"Yeah right! All of you say that shit, but it's probably a few of you right now who are sitting up in here waiting for your HIV test results to come back. Some of you are talking about, 'Oh God, please don't let my shit come back positive. I promise I won't bone again without my jimmy. Oh God, please!'"* Everybody laughed because they knew he was telling the truth.

"I say that for real though. If you don't use protection you already got AIDS. That stands for...Ain't

Ignorant (just) Damn Stupid!" Everybody laughed and applauded.

"Brothers. Oh, my brothers. We have been on the sisters for too long about the weave thang. It's cool now to have somebody else's hair on your head. Hell, even Toni Braxton has gone to the weave. It's time the sisters step to the brothers about these bald heads." The ladies in the crowd started clapping their hands.

"It sure is time!" shouted one lady.

Special K continued with his point, *"Brothers read my lips -- some of you don't look good with a bald head. QUIT SHAVING YOUR SHIT IF YOU GOT A FUCKED UP HEAD! Don't do it! It ain't gonna make you look like Michael Jordan. Your baldheaded-ass head might look like a monkey's balls -- but not like Mike!"*

"I saw this one brother the other day and his head looked like an elbow. It had all kinda dents and wrinkles in it. What really tripped me out was, it had a dark ring that sloped down right in the back of his head. Tell me, why would a brother want to shave his head and show all that shit? I just don't understand!"

The crowd's laughter was endless. In fact, Kayra laughed so hard she felt herself needing to pee. "Pam I need to go to the restroom, do you want to come?"

"No, go on. I'm staying to watch the show. He's so funny!"

"Okay, I'll be right back." Kayra got up and walked quickly toward the back in the direction of the bar, which was near the restroom. When she got a few feet from the table, she felt her bladder about to explode! By the time she got near the bar, she broke into a full sprint and ran right past Jake. She didn't see him at all. Luckily for him because he was hugged up with Yolanda, who by this time was kissing all over him.

As soon as Kayra was out of sight in the bathroom, a couple who had been seated behind her and Pam's table got up and left. When they did, Pam turned around and there he was. Jake the snake! He was in plain view. Pam didn't recognize him at first. The two previous times they had met, all she did was check out his "A.C.". She turned back around and continued listening to *Special K*'s last few minutes on stage. Then she thought for a few seconds and turned back around to look. *"I know him from somewhere."* Just at that moment, Yolanda leaned over to Jake and gave him a long sloppy kiss. When she stopped, Pam saw Jake's face again, but she still couldn't place him.

Jake stood up. "Yolanda, I got to go to the little boy's room. I'll be right back, baby."

"Can I come?" asked Yolanda.

Jake laughed, "No sweetheart, not this time. When I get you home, you can do whatever you want!"

When he turned around and headed for the back. Pam looked at his ass and said, "Oh, my God! That's Jim -- John -- or whatever his name is. That low-down motherfucker! He was supposed to be with Kayra tonight, now he's with that whore!"

Pam realized how loud she was and people were starting to look at her. She stopped talking and waved for a waiter.

"Yes, can I help you?"

"Yes, you can!" Pam took out some paper and a pen. She wrote a note that said. *'You no good bastard!'* "Here, take this over to that bastard over there at the bar with the lady in the gold dress," said Pam giving the paper to the waiter.

"Yes."

"Thank you."

The waiter left the table just as Kayra came back to sit down.

"Did I miss anything?" asked Kayra.

Pam rolled her eyes. "You damn sure did!"

♥

Jake returned to his seat and got comfortable with Yolanda. The waiter gave him the folded piece of paper from Pam.

"What do you have there, man?" asked Malik. "You got another woman sending you love notes. I told you Yolanda, you'd better hold on to him."

"Don't worry, I will!"

"Let me see here," said Jake while opening the note. *You no good bastard*! He read. "Hey, what is this?" He signaled the waiter back to the bar. "Who sent this?" The waiter leaned over and pointed to Pam and Kayra's table. "I don't see anybody," questioned Jake.

"Well sir, she must be gone," replied the waiter.

Jake quickly pushed Yolanda away from him.

"We've gotta go baby!" He and Yolanda stood up and turned around. Pam and Kayra were standing right behind them.

"Too late! Your ass is busted!" shouted Pam.

Jake almost fell down in shock. Malik looked up and saw what was going on.

"Damn! Run Jake!"

Instead, Jake tried to play it off by being polite.

"Hi, Kayra, I didn't know you were coming out tonight."

"I bet you didn't. Who is this?" asked Kayra.

Jake turned to her, but he really didn't know what to say.

"This is just a friend of mine. Her name is Yolanda." He turned to try and introduce them.

Yolanda quickly stopped him.

"I don't want to meet your damn...."

Pam suddenly stepped in and yelled, "Fuck you bitch! And you, you punk ass no good nigger! You got some nerve standing my girl up, then coming out with this whore!"

"I ain't no damn whore!"

"Shut up bitch, before I knock your ass out!" yelled Pam.

"Look Yolanda, just be cool!" insisted Jake as Kayra finally spoke up.

"Pam, I can handle this!" yelled Kayra.

"Handle your business then, girl!" replied Pam.

"Jake, I thought you were different, but you're just like all the rest of those lying ass niggers I've dealt with. You could have been honest enough to let me know you were still dating other people. Your ass lied about tonight!"

"I didn't lie, there's Malik!"

Kayra looked over at Malik hugged up with Nicole as he waved at her with a silly ass grin on his face.

"Yeah, I can see you two are really bonding like old friends. Look, you keep having your fun. I don't want to ever see you again! Ever! Let's go Pam."

Kayra and Pam rushed out the club while Jake was left standing with a bewildered look on his face. As they headed towards the door, Pam turned back and saw Jake. She gave him "the finger" and lipped "fuck you!"

Malik and Nicole stood up. "What's up, man? asked Malik. "You went from sugar to shit!"

"Shut up!" demanded Jake.

"Jake, be straight up with me. Was that your woman?" asked Yolanda.

"No, she is not my woman. I told you, she is just a friend or at least she was." lied Jake.

"Well, your friend seemed to be very upset and ready to kick your ass! I should be mad at you, too. That's okay, I learned to expect this kind of shit from men. You always want some pussy on the side and end up getting your asses busted! Then you get mad and try to turn the shit around to make it seem like it's our fault. *WHAT MEN DON'T UNDERSTAND IS, IF THEY HANDLED THEIR BUSINESS AT HOME AND THOUGHT WITH THEIR HEADS INSTEAD OF THEIR DICKS, THEY MIGHT BE ABLE TO KEEP A GOOD WOMAN.* That's not to say some women aren't full of shit too. The difference is, we're not stupid like men. We know how to play the game. Men just let their egos tell them they can do anything, anywhere. And now you see what happens when they do! I ain't mad at you Jake, because I'm not a 'player hater' but a 'player congratulator,'" smiled Yolanda. "Come on, I'm ready to go home."

"Here Malik," said Jake as threw him the keys to his car. "I'm going to ride with Yolanda. You can drive my car home tonight, but be careful! I'll come by tomorrow to pick it up."

"Alright, my brother. Are you going to be cool?"

"Yeah, see ya!"

Chapter 5

*T*he trip home was filled with, Pam and Kayra's talk of what a dog Jake had been and how men kept finding ways to disappoint them.

"I can't believe he would do this to me," cried Kayra.

"I do!" replied Pam. "It's the same old thing all the time. They sweeten you up with all their smooth talking, then once they feel you're under their spell, the real them starts to slowly appear. The bad thing about it is, by the time they've turned into this other person, you're already set up for heartbreak. It's so true what they say, *the man you meet on Saturday, ain't the same nigger you end up with on Sunday.*"

"You're right Pam, I should have learned my lesson from dealing with the other losers I've had. Now this happens! Anyway, how is it that you know so much about men? I don't ever remember you running to me with a man problem."

"Well Kayra, let's just say I've had my share of let downs. And since the last one, I've decided to start dishing out more shit than I take!"

The two women sat quietly on Pam's white, bear-skinned rug in front of the large crackling fireplace, while they listened to Pam's *Love Jones soundtrack* CD, which was smooth as shit. "How about a little night cap?" asked Pam. "It will help you relax."

"I don't know—well, why not?" replied Kayra.

Pam got up and went into the kitchen. She carefully filled two small glasses with ice and poured a generous amount of cognac in both of them. She went back into the den, sat down and gave Kayra her glass.

"Let's make a toast! *Here's to all the dog ass men in our lives. May they never hurt us again.*"

"*Oh, and may they forever step in their own shit!*" added Kayra.

"Hmmm, Pam this is good! What is it?"

"Cognac. You're not supposed to drink it with ice, only at room temperature, but I didn't think you were ready for that—it's an acquired taste," answered Pam.

Kayra lifted her glass and took another big sip. "I guess I better slow down before I get myself into more trouble than I'm already in."

"Don't worry Kayra, you're at home. As a matter of fact, why don't you spend the night? It will be fun. Besides, it's Friday night after 1:00 a.m., and I don't feel like taking you home. See, I told you when you moved here to Chicago to just stay with me for a while, but no you insisted on getting your own place."

"It's not like that and you know it. I came to Chicago to stand on my own two feet and besides I needed my space.

"Yeah, sure you did. I know what a big social life you have," laughed Pam.

"Ha, ha, Pam. Very funny."

"So, are you staying or what?"

"Okay, I'll stay here and relax. We haven't had a sleep over in years."

"Good!" replied Pam. "First, let's get out of these clothes and I'll get us some pajamas. Then we'll come back to finish the bottle of cognac. It will be just you and me in front of the fireplace."

Pam and Kayra quickly got comfortable. When they were settled on the floor, they each returned to sipping their drinks.

"Isn't that good? It's almost better than sex!"

"Hell, no!" laughed Kayra. "But seriously, thanks for being here for me when I needed you. I don't know what I would have done if you hadn't."

"Girl, don't worry about all the "thank u's", replied Pam.

Kayra thought about how messed up the night had been. But before long, she and Pam found themselves laughing, joking and gossiping all night long. For the moment, Kayra and Pam felt closer than ever. It was the first time they'd spent quality time together in almost five years. By the time they finished talking, their drinks were gone and the fire had dwindled away. They lay silently together and held each other until they drifted off to sleep. It was a magical experience neither would soon forget.

♥

When morning came, Pam was eager to get the day started with Kayra.

"What do you feel like doing?" asked Pam.

"I don't know."

"Well, there is always plenty of shopping to do!" Pam excitedly suggested.

"No more shopping, thank you very much!" replied Kayra quickly.

"How about we don't do anything and stay here? To be honest with you, I'm not up for much right now anyway, including shopping!" said Pam.

"Now that's a first!" said Kayra laughing.

"You know what you can kiss!" joked Pam.

"Now that wasn't nice. But I'm not going to pay you any attention. Look, I had so much fun last night, I was wondering if I can stay a few more days. At least, until I get a grip on all this. Also, I want to avoid Jake, just in case he decides to come to my house or call...that is, if he's not having too much fun with his new bitch!"

"Believe me Kayra, one of these days he'll know what a good woman he missed!"

Chapter 6

*M*alik sat quietly as he and Nicole pulled in the driveway of his townhouse.

"What's wrong?" asked Nicole as she gently rubbed the back of his neck to smooth out whatever might be on his mind.

"Nothing's wrong Nicole. It's just after all the shit that happened tonight, I'm getting kinda worried."

"Worried about what?" asked Nicole. "Is it Jake? If it is, I'll just say this. I know he's your friend and all, but if he lied to that girl and tried to dog her out, I think he got what he deserved."

"No, it's not just about Jake."

"What then?"

"Well, it's like this Nicole. I like you a lot and I want to have a relationship with you."

"How do you know that? Do you think you know me already?"

"Yes, I do as a matter of fact. When we talk, I feel we're on the same side about issues. For example, you are a sister who understands what it takes for a strong black man to make it these days. More importantly, you know what your role, as a black woman should be. It's not just about being submissive, by no means. It's about being supportive. Nicole, you are independent and self-assured. To me you exemplify all the beauty of a black woman both inside and out."

"Hold up, Malik! I appreciate all you're saying, but please don't move us to a long and happy life together after meeting me only a few hours ago. I'll admit, we do hit it off good, but I'm not ready for anything serious right now, which is where I think you're going with all this. Let's take our time, get to know each other, and we'll see what happens. Is that alright?"

"Cool." answered Malik.

"Now, can we please get out of this car before I suffocate. This heater is blowing full blast right in my face!"

Malik didn't say a word. He felt kinda stupid for pouring his heart out to Nicole. *"But at least I'm getting laid!"* he chuckled to himself.

"What are you mumbling about, Malik?"

"Oh, nothing, it's an inside joke!"

♥

Jake and Yolanda finally spoke after a long silent ride to Jake's house from the club.

"Do you want something to drink?" asked Jake, in his most seducing voice. "It's been a long night and I thought it would be nice to relax with a hot cup of coffee."

"Well, it is kinda chilly in here," replied Yolanda.

"Yes, it is, and it ain't from the weather!" mumbled Jake, referring to Yolanda's sudden lack of affection. Eventually she loosened up, took her shoes off, and walked to the couch to curl up.

"Do you have a blanket I can have?" asked Yolanda.

"Yes." Jake opened the closet, pulled out a large wool blanket and gave it to Yolanda.

"Thank you. I apologize for snapping at you earlier."

"That's okay, I understand," answered Jake, surprised by Yolanda's sudden apology. "You have a right to be mad after all that happened tonight. I'm really sorry for putting you through all that drama! How can I make it up to you?"

"Well, you can light the fireplace and bring your sexy self over here next to me and keep me warm."

"I guess you still want a little sumthin', sumthin'!" replied Jake, as he walked to the couch to Yolanda.

Without saying a word, she reached and grabbed Jake's penis.

"No. What I'm saying is, I want a lot of sumthin', sumthin'!"

"Oh, I can handle that!" Jake quickly replied. "Damn, I hear the pot whistling. Let me go fix your coffee, and then I'll light the fireplace." Jake ran into the kitchen and quickly poured Yolanda's coffee.

"Would you like cream and sugar?" he asked loudly from the kitchen.

"Just sugar for now. I'll get the cream when I get finish with you!"

"Oh shit!" yelled Jake, running back into the living room. He looked at Yolanda sitting on the couch butt naked. Her fine body calling for him to come take it. "I thought you were cold?"

"I was, until I started getting wet thinking about you."

"Here's your coffee."

"Thank you."

"Now, let me get that fire going."

"It already is!" replied Yolanda smiling and licking her lips slowly with her tongue while she rubbed between her thighs.

Jake was in such a hurry to start the fire, he damn near burned down the house until he finally got things under control. By that time, Yolanda had laid down across the couch with her legs spread wide open.

Jake walked away from the fireplace to the couch. He slowly undressed while he watched Yolanda caress herself until she almost had an orgasm. He then eased himself on top of her. Yolanda felt his large chest and swollen manhood rubbing against her throbbing body. Jake kissed her around the neck, then on her breast. When he put his lips on her nipples, they grew like large fruits of desire. He stuck his tongue out and licked down her stomach until he reached between her creamy thighs, where he stayed inside her until she screamed with excitement. He stopped, moved back up her body and penetrated her. They made sex for the rest of the night before they collapsed in each other's arms.

Chapter 7

*T*he morning started early for Jake and Yolanda, after their night of hot passion.

Jake decided since it was early Saturday morning, he might be able to catch his son Railey at home. It had been two months since he had spoken to him, or his mother Indigo.

Over the years Jake and Indigo had entertained the idea of getting back together and on occasion they even had some wild nights of romance. Reluctantly, they both decided (for Railey's sake) that it would be better if they only remained friends.

"Jake, where are you going? It's too early to get up. Lie down and just hold me," pleaded Yolanda.

"I'm going to use the phone to call Railey."

"Who?"

"My son!" answered Jake angerily.

"I didn't know you had a son. How old is he?"

"He's ten."

"What happened to you and his mother?"

"Wait a minute. Wait just one minute! What's with all the questions? All I said was, I'll be right back, I have to use the phone. The next thing I know, I'm getting a bunch of questions."

"Excuse me, Jake for trying to show some interest in your ass! You don't have to get all defensive about the shit."

Jake stood up and put on the silk robe laying on the bed.

"I'm sorry. I wasn't trying to trip," he replied. Then he explained the deal with him and Indigo. "He doesn't live with me. His mother and I broke up a long time ago and we thought it would be better if he stayed with her. Now that he's older, he spends the summers and every other Christmas with me."

"What happened between you and what's her name?"

"Indigo."

"That's a very pretty name. Anyway, what happened with Indigo? Were you dating for a while before the split?"

"Well, as a matter of fact, we were married for three years until things started to deteriorate for various reasons. The time came when we just called it quits! Now are you satisfied?"

Yolanda sat back on the bed quietly.

"Mr. Alexander, there's a lot I have to find out about you. You are full of surprises!"

Jake left the bedroom without saying a word, only smiling as he went into the den to use the phone.

"I sure hope he's home. Come on, pick up the phone somebody."

"Hello."

"Hello, Indigo?"

"Yes, this is she."

"What's up? This is Jake, how are you doing?"

"Hi, Jake, I'm doing fine. What are you doing calling this early? Where are you? We haven't heard from you in a couple of months."

"I'm sorry, I've been busy with the stores. You know how crazy things can get. What about you, how have you been?"

"I've been fine, I've just gotten over a little cold."

"How's the job coming?" asked Jake.

"Oh, I just got promoted to vice-president of advertising."

"Get outta here!" shouted Jake surprised by the news. "Congratulations! I wish I was there to give you a little loving to help you celebrate!" said Jake in his patented sexy voice.

Indigo laughed and replied, "I bet you do, and the way I've been feeling, you probably couldn't hang. I've been so horny!"

Jake looked around and made sure Yolanda wasn't listening. "Now you know I'd wear your ass out! You and I, we got it like that! Besides, I still love you."

"We'd better cut this out," said Indigo, as she started getting excited. "You want to talk to your son? I hope that's why you really called."

"Thanks, put him on. Bye!"

Indigo gave the phone to Railey who was standing next to her pulling on her shirttail asking who it was?

"Hello," he said with the phone firmly pressed against his little cheek.

"Hi, son. How are you?" asked Jake.

"Hi daddy," said Railey, excited once he was able to recognize Jake's voice. "I'm fine, daddy."

"Have you been a good boy?"

"Yes, I've been real good. I met a new friend named Erik. He has a frog named Sam."

"He does, huh?" asked Jake.

"Yeah, and I play with it sometimes, but not anymore because we had him in our house and he got lost. That made mama real mad!"

"I bet it did! Next time be more careful, okay?"

"Okay, daddy."

"Is there anything you want me to send you?"

59

"Yeah, you can send me one of those new turtle man outfits and some new skates. All the other kids got some but me. They make fun of me and try to make me mad because they know I don't have any."

"Why doesn't your mother just buy you some?"

"Because she's triflin'!"

"What do you mean triflin'? Where did you hear that word from?"

"From mama, while she was talking to her friend," answered Railey, as if Jake had just asked him a dumb question.

"Don't use that word again until you get grown. You understand?

"Yes...sir."

"Okay. Well, I got to go now," said Jake eagerly trying to get off the phone.

"I love you, dad."

"I love you too," replied Jake.

Afterwards, Jake hung up the phone and walked back to the bedroom. Yolanda was waiting for him to bring her some more loving.

"Come here, Jake. I'm glad you're finally off the phone because I got something to give you!"

"What do you have to give me?" asked Jake, while taking off his rope.

Yolanda slowly removed the sheets from her naked body and spread her legs wide open. "I got this to give you," pointing to her wet, pink kitten. Jake smiled and the two of them made sex for another two hours.

When they finally decided to come up for air, Yolanda laid in bed trying to recover from the exhausting sex feast. Jake remained distant and didn't want to talk, so Yolanda decided to try and break the ice.

"Did you enjoy talking to your son?"

"I sure did. I really miss him a lot! It's hard being a long distance father. I miss a lot of his life. Children need the interaction with both parents. Anyway, didn't you say you had some more for me?" asked Jake trying to change the subject. Yolanda nodded her head and immediately Jake mounted her again. They made sex once more until it was noon.

After he and Yolanda finished, Jake thought about Kayra and how much he must have hurt her. He was crazy about her—even though she could never replace or measure up to the love he and Indigo shared. In his heart, Jake felt love was never as good as the first time. He also knew he didn't mean for things to turn out like they had with Kayra. He really wanted to have a relationship with her. *"But look what happened! I lose Kayra and end up with Yolanda the skeezer!"* he thought. Jake decided he was going to mend things with Kayra. *"The first step is to get rid of Yolanda."*

Yolanda saw the distant look on Jake's face.

"What are your plans for the day?" asked Yolanda.

"I don't know Yolanda. I got a couple of meetings to go to."

"Do you want me to wait for you?"

"No, you just go on home. I'll call you later," replied Jake quickly, to stop any more of Yolanda's ideas to get with him.

"Sounds like you're ready for me to leave!" proclaimed Yolanda, upset by Jake's sudden change of attitude.

"It's not like that. I just got a few things I need to do and I know with your fine ass here, I'm not going to get anything done!"

"Well, I guess I'll give you a break. I know you're a busy man and all! Will you please go get me a towel? I'll shower and be on my way."

"Two towels coming right up!"

Before Jake turned to go get the towels, Yolanda reached and started slowly rubbing Jake's penis again.

"Are you sure we don't have a few more minutes to spare?"

Jake moved her hand and jumped out the bed before he found himself hard again and climbing right back on top of her.

"Let me get those towels now!"

Disappointed, Yolanda hit the bed hard with her fist. Then she got up, took a shower, and dressed.

"Jake, I'm ready to go! Thanks for a real good time last night and today."

"Thank you, Yolanda. I really enjoyed your company. I'm sorry for all the trouble I put you through."

"Sure you are!" answered Yolanda smiling. "When will I see you again?"

"We'll get together soon. I promise."

"Okay!" said Yolanda, as if unsatisfied by Jake's answer, but she decided not to push the issue. Instead, she gave him a kiss and headed out the door.

Jake watched as she climbed into her car and drove off into the foggy morning.

"Whew, I'm glad that's over with. She was about to fuck me to death! Now I got to call Kayra. I hope she's at home." Jake stumbled around looking for the phone. "Where is that motherf...? There it is!" He grabbed the phone off the floor and dialed Kayra's house.

"Damn! No answer."

Just before he hung up the phone, Kayra's voice mail picked up.

"Hello this is Kayra."

"Hi, Kayra."

"I'm sorry, I'm not here to receive your call. If you leave your name, number and a brief message, I promise to get back with you as soon as possible." Beep..Beep...Beep

"Damn, ain't this a bitch! Her monkey ass ain't even at home!" Jake thought maybe he should leave a message. "I'd better not. I don't want to give her any warning. If I catch her off guard, maybe she'll listen to what I have to say."

"Well, I wonder how Malik is making it. Let me give him a call. I need to get my car from him anyway."

"Hello," answered a low voice, still half asleep.

"Malik, this is Jake. What's up?"

"Nothing's up, what time is it?" asked Malik while trying to wipe the sleep from his eyes.

"It's twelve o'clock noon or something like that and you're not up yet?" replied Jake laughing. He knew Malik was a late sleeper and hated to be bothered anytime before two o'clock.

"No, Nicole and I went at it all night long! You know how that is." said Malik, as if he was actually used to getting laid. The fact of the matter was, he hadn't had pussy since pussy had him!

Jake heard Nicole giggling softly in the background.

"Yeah, I know how it is. When are you going to make a move? I need to get my car."

"Give me until three o'clock. I'll drop Nicole off and then I'll swoop by your crib."

"Alright, cool man. Three o'clock. Be here!"

Jake laughed to himself and laid back on the bed. In the silence of the house, he began to reminisce about all of his past relationships. How he used to fall in and out of love so fast he couldn't keep up with what was real and what was not. He thought about all the hearts he had broken and the terrible ways he had treated women when he was in college.

Then there was Indigo, the mother of his child and his ex-wife. What a wonderful relationship they had. They were the best of friends and great lovers. Most of all, they were excellent parents to their son, Railey. They had some very rough times together and their share of arguments, until they let the relationship end without putting in the effort to make it work. After all these years, he thought he had changed. Now it seemed as if he was still the same old Jake. "The shit always ended up the same damn way. Somebody gotta get hurt, and I'm usually the one doing all the hurting."

♥

Malik finally showed up to Jake's house eagerly waiting to tell him all about his night with Nicole. He rang the door bell. "Where the hell is that Negro at?"

Startled, Jake shook his head to wake up and then he looked at the clock which read three o'clock.

"Damn! That's probably Malik. I must have fallen asleep. Malik kept knocking on the door. "Okay! Okay! I'm coming!"

Malik stopped knocking and Jake finally answered the door. "Come on in man." he invited.

"You're not even ready." observed Malik.

"Ready for what?"

"I assumed you were going somewhere, since you were hurrying for me to come get you."

"No, I just wanted my car so when I'm ready to make a move I won't have to wait on you! Does that clear it up for you?"

"I guess, if you're gonna play a brother like that!"

"Good! Now have a seat my brother and make yourself at home. How are you and Nicole?"

"What do you mean?"

"You know what I mean. Are you in love yet?"

"Oh man, why does it have to be all that?"

"I was checking out how 'lovey dovey' you two were last night."

"I know you didn't go there! After you and Yolanda were practically fucking at the club. Plus, I won't even go into you getting busted!" Jake and Malik both burst out laughing.

"But for real, how is Kay..Karen?"

"Her name is Kayra. And I don't know how she's doing. I haven't talked to her."

"Man, I think you messed up big time! From the looks of things, you hurt her pretty bad. She might not ever want to talk to your ass again!"

"I know!" said Jake putting his head down. "You're right, she might not ever want to talk to me again. But I've got to keep trying. I need to tell her how much I care about her and that I didn't mean to hurt her."

"You honestly think she's gonna believe that shit after what you put her through last night?"

Jake looked at Malik and shook his head. "Gee thanks. You're sure a comfort to have around!"

"What are you going to do about Yolanda?" asked Malik trying to make a point. "It would be my guess that you probably got her nose wide open too! If you diss her you're probably going to end up with the same drama you did with Kayra last night. Just face it man, you're a dangerous brother when it comes to women. I know you don't intend for it to be like that, but if I was a woman, I would stay as far away from your ass as I could! I know that sounds cold, but it's the truth!"

Jake was so convicted by what Malik said, he couldn't say a word to the contrary. All he did was pick up the phone and make another call to Kayra's house. This time he had made up his mind to leave a message on her answering machine.

"*Hello this is Kayra, I'm not at home to receive... Beep..Beep..*" The machine stopped before Jake realized it and he found himself not knowing what to say.

"*Hi, Kayra. I want you to know that I am very sorry for everything that has happened and I would like to...* Beep..Beep..Beep. The machine cut him off before he finished his message. "*Damn, it cut me off!*" Jake slammed the phone down angrily.

"What's wrong?" asked Malik.

"Kayra's freakin' answering machine cut me off before I could tell her to call me."

"Well call her back!"

"I don't know, I might sound........ you know."

"Man, call her back!" demanded Malik.

"Alright!"

After dailing Kayra's phone number, Jake waited to hear the machine pickup. He quickly barked, "*Kayra, call me!*" and then he hung up the phone.

Chapter 8

*W*hile Jake was busy leaving messages at Kayra's house, she was busy chillin' out with Pam who had decided to pamper her with a warm bubble bath.

"Your water is ready."

"Pam, you really don't have to do this for me."

"I know, but I want to. I keep telling you, what are friends for?"

"Pam, thanks again," said Kayra, as she went into the bathroom to take off the silk pajamas Pam had given her last night. Pam watched and smiled as Kayra slowly walked to the tub and sunk her naked body into the warm bubbles. Pam thought to herself how beautiful Kayra's body was and how stupid men must be to treat her the way they do. As far as she was concerned, Kayra had the looks, body, and personality to make her desirable to anyone with half a brain.

"They don't deserve her!" thought Pam to herself. *"If they don't know how to treat her then they*

shouldn't have her." From that moment on, Pam promised herself she wasn't going to let another man come into Kayra's life to hurt her.

♥

Kayra settled into the steamy romantic bath Pam had drawn for her. It was peaceful yet rejuvenating. She allowed the soft, sweet-smelling water to completely cover her. She laid her head back on the inflated pillow and closed her eyes. Cunningly, Pam walked in with a sponge scrubber. Kayra opened her eyes and saw Pam standing over her. She was startled by her presence.

"I'm sorry, I didn't mean to scare you, Kayra. I see you are still tense and uptight. Let me wash your back for you. It will relax those nerves of yours!"

"That sounds wonderful. I am still a little tense, replied Kayra. Pam bent to her knees and lathered up the sponge and began to gently scrub Kayra's back. Kayra closed her eyes again and let the moment take her away. She moaned under her breath when Pam started to massage her neck and shoulders. Pam slowly moved down Kayra's back with the skill of a masseuse.

"How did you learn to do this so well?" asked Kayra enjoyably.

"Oh, it's just a little something I picked up from an old friend!" answered Pam.

"It sure feels good. You be sure to tell that old friend of yours that they taught you well!"

"I'm glad you are enjoying it," laughed Pam.

"Why don't you finish this up and I'll be right back."

"Make it quick!" said Kayra as she continued to bathe herself.

♥

In the living room Pam thought how comfortable Kayra was with her. *"How nice it would be, if it was just the two of us forever instead of putting up with all the bullshit from men."* Pam convinced herself that she could make Kayra happier than any man ever could. *"I would be her friend, companion and even her lover! But how can I tell her? I don't want to frighten her into rejecting me."*

The past twenty-four hours with Kayra had planted a passion in Pam's heart that transcended the boundaries of mere friendship. Pam came to terms with the fact that she had fallen in love with Kayra. They had always shared a sisterly love for one another. Pam, however, had had passionate feelings for Kayra the past ten years but never wanted to discuss it with her. Pam just tried to hide her true feelings, and now that had to stop! She went into the closet, grabbed a large towel and returned to the bathroom with Kayra.

"I'm back," announced Pam as Kayra sported a big smile on her face without saying a word. "Are you through bathing?"

"Yes. I guess I'd better get out before I shrivel up like a prune," laughed Kayra.

"You're right! Come on over here and let me dry you off."

"You don't have to do that," replied Kayra feeling something was up.

"Girl, what did I tell you earlier about that?"

"I know, I know!"

Kayra got out of the tub covered with bubbles over her smooth body. Pam unfolded the huge towel and stretched it out as far as she could. Kayra looked very uncomfortable as she eased over to Pam. She stood and shivered as Pam dried her body with the soft towel.

"Relax Kayra, I'm not going to hurt you. I never want you to be hurt ever again. Please, don't be afraid of me." Pam continued drying Kayra's back, then her breast, holding them firmly with the towel as Kayra jumped.

"Pam, what do you think you're doing?"

"You like that don't you?" whispered Pam in Kayra's ear while she rubbed her breast faster and started kissing her on the neck. Kayra started breathing harder and then she began to moan.

"I've been wanting to tell you something, but I don't know how to say it," whispered Pam again in Kayra's ear.

She turned and held Pam's hand firmly.

"Just please say it, Pam. You can tell me anything."

Pam looked Kayra in the eyes.

"I've been in love with you for years!" Silently, Kayra slowly loosened her grip of Pam's hand. "Yes Kayra, I just never knew how to tell you."

Kayra grabbed Pam's hands and pulled her into her arms. They looked into each other's eyes and smiled. Pam dropped the towel from Kayra's naked body and teased her nipples with her tongue. Kayra unfastened Pam's robe and dropped it to the floor. They stood in front of each other naked and confused about what was happening.

"Are you okay with this?"

"Yes, Pam. I'm okay!"

Pam reached out to Kayra and led her hand in hand into the bedroom, where they made love for hours. When they finished, they lay still—both looking like they could use a cigarette. Each tried to express her feelings, but the words just kept getting in the way. For a moment, Kayra felt Pam had gotten her into another situation that she should not have been in. But the fact was, Kayra was already in love with Pam and too afraid to admit it. Now the question was, how would this affect their friendship? Neither Pam, nor Kayra had an answer for the time being. Instead they cuddled and held each other as tears rolled from their eyes like bottles at sea with messages. Each tear telling a story of its own, soaking the bed linen with emotions.

Both Pam and Kayra knew that men had led them to this experience between them. Because of them, Kayra acted on the taboo of being with Pam. Now she could answer the questions for herself. *"Could a man's negligence toward his woman be why she would be pushed to love and long for the affection of another woman? Are failed relationships with the opposite sex the cause of growth in our gay and lesbian society?"* thought Kayra.

Pam and Kayra wondered if this would be the end of their involvement with men. Although Pam had had these feelings for a while, this was her first time being with a woman—at least that's what she told Kayra who hadn't come to terms with her desires for either sex. She had always reacted strictly based on emotions. When she met Jake, it was the first time she really felt tuned in and emotionally stimulated. This thing with Pam was beyond any and everything she had ever dreamed possible. If they could only freeze this moment for the rest of their lives.

"Kayra, before this goes any further than it already has, well I guess it couldn't go much further-- anyway, I don't want to take advantage of you, while you're going through this shit with Jake. Seeing you hurt and broken-hearted helped me to realize that I should let you know how I feel."

"Pam, you don't have to explain. I know you've always cared deeply for me and would never take advantage of me. I've always known I felt attracted to you. We've shared a lot together and I can honestly say I have no regrets about what we did. You know, this did happen so fast and made things seem out of control. First, it was the stuff with Jake. Then I come here and end up in bed with you! What am I supposed to do?" sighed Kayra.

"What do you want to do?"

"Damn it Pam, I don't know!"

"Take your time, Kayra. You don't have to make any decisions right now. I can understand how this must be taking a toll on you. After all, this is new to me too! You know, with us being friends and lovers. Despite what you might think, I'm not gay. I mean, I have never been with another woman before because you know I love me some dick! What I don't love is what's attached to it! That's a problem I'm ready to start dealing with. I'm just like you, I'm not sure what to do or where we go from here? I don't want this to ruin our friendship. I do know that!"

"Don't worry, it won't Pam." Kayra reached and rubbed Pam's cheeks. "I'd better go now."

"You don't have to leave. I thought you were going to stay a couple of more days," said Pam, very upset.

"I know, but I think it would be best if I went home and had time to myself. Maybe it will help me put all this in perspective. I told you Pam, I'm not going to stop loving you nor be angry with you. I just want some time to think, that's all!"

Pam leaned over and kissed Kayra passionately. When she finished, she told Kayra to leave and take as much time as she needed. Kayra got up, took a shower and dressed. She thanked Pam for a wonderful time and for being a good friend. They hugged and were careful not to say the wrong thing—didn't want to spark any tears.

"Bye." said Kayra while planting a kiss on Pam's forehead.

"Bye," replied Pam, trying to hold back the tear that was hanging in the corner of her eye. She stood in the doorway until Kayra was long out of sight, and then she burst out into tears.

Chapter 9

*J*ake signaled to Malik that it was time to go.
 "Hold up Jake, let's sit down for a minute.
I'm your boy and I beleive you haven't told me
everything about you and this Kayra chick. If you really
want her back, you have got to take a hard look at
yourself."
 "What do you mean?"
 "I know you and I see the same pattern.
Look at how you treat women. I'm not saying you're a
bad person. You're really a good brother at heart. You're
just like a lot of us who have a problem keeping our
dicks in our pants! We can love our woman to death,
but if another one shakes her ass the right way, we go
temporarily insane! Next thing you know, we're cheating
just to get a little "piece" on the side. Quiet as it's kept,
this isn't just a black man's problem, but men period!
There are women who are just as scandalous, although
men get all the bad press. It still doesn't give us an

excuse to act like whores and try to fuck every woman who opens her legs. It's not just about that these days. Diseases are going around killing brothers left and right. I'm sorry I got to break it down like this, but if I can't be real with you, what do we have as friends?"

"You sure had a mouthful on your mind! As bad as I hate to support your philosophical theory on the behavior of men, I can't ignore the fact that you're right! However, most of the time I get the short end of the stick. I'm not saying I wasn't wrong for some of the things I did, but I never abused or misused anybody. I sincerely thought I'd changed and was finally becoming the man I had always wanted to be. Now this happens! Here I was talking about your ass with the black shit, and I should've been checking to see where my head was."

Malik got out of his chair and walked to the window. He gazed at the beautiful scenery of the sun's rays gleaming off the lake that surrounds Jake's house.

"My, what a beautiful view you got here, man," observed Malik, as if he wasn't listening to Jake.

"Have you heard a word I've said? You suppose to be my man and you seem like you playin' me to the left!"

"I'm not playing you at all. I'm trying to get you to check yourself! What kind of example are you setting for Railey? He sees his daddy in all these different relationships, which means he has to keep dealing with different women strolling in and out of his life. Man, the shit gets deep, whether you know it or not. You never know what will have a lasting affect on a child's life when the child gets older."

"What can I do?"

"Be real with yourself! You need to check out who Jake really is, and what Jake wants and needs in a woman. Then pray to God and ask him to send her to you."

"Oh, so God is going to pop a woman in my bed and say, *whomp, there she is!*" Jake laughed so hard, he rolled back on the couch holding his stomach. Malik tried to keep a straight face but couldn't. He giggled and continued trying to make his point to Jake.

"I don't know if praying works, but that's what my mama always told me. I'm not religious and all that. Hell, I haven't stepped foot in a church in about two or three years, but I've come to realize that you do need God in your life to make things work." preached Jake.

"I know what you mean. It's been a while for me too!" amened Malik.

Malik and Jake were momentarily quiet. They looked out the window and watched it begin to snow, as the sun faded away into the bosom of the awaiting clouds.

"Why don't we go to church this Sunday?" asked Malik. "God only knows we both need it. Especially you!"

"Very funny!" replied Jake. "The walls might start shaking if I come through the doors, but I don't need to hear it from you. Besides, I need to wait until I get my shit together."

"I feel the same way. But mama said the Bible teaches us to *come as we are*. I take that to mean, come no matter what's going on in your life."

Jakes nervously paced the floor and decided he'd had enough of the conversation. "Alright, we'll go. What have I got to lose? Now let's get outta here. I want to see if I can catch Kayra at home—since she's not answering her phone."

"Man, you need to leave that girl alone for now. Give her some time to get herself together! If you go over there like some cowboy, all you're going to do is piss her off, and you might not ever be able to talk to her again."

"Why don't you go with me?"

"I'm not going over there and let her cuss me out! You clean up your own shit. You're my man, but I don't feel like fuckin' around and gettin' in the middle of you and Kayra's bullshit."

Jake tried to talk Malik into changing his mind, but to no avail. "All I want you to do is be there for me. You don't have to do any talking, lying, or none of that shit! You sat up in here and told me how fucked up I was and now you won't even help a brother."

"You didn't have to go there!" replied Malik throwing up his hands.

"Yeah, I'm gonna go there. You know you wrong. You know I wouldn't ask if it didn't mean a lot to me. I always got your back!"

"I got your back too, but you're trying to get me in that domestic nonsense."

"Just do me this one favor man. You know how I feel about Kayra. I need her back and I don't want to lose her!"

Malik walked up to Jake and looked him in the eyes.

"What are you saying, Jake? Are you too embarrassed to look at me?"

"I told you before, I think I'm in love with her!"

"Oh no! If you ask me, I think you're trying to replace Indigo. That's just me and my opinion. Either way you look at it, you should forget about going to Kayra's house!"

Jake turned and walked silently to the door with his feelings hurt.

"I'll do it!" mumbled Malik.

"Excuse me, what did you say?" replied Jake.

"I said, I'll go over to Kayra's house with you," said Malik walking outside to the car. "But if she starts trippin', we're leavin' with the quickness!"

"Okay let's go!" said Jake, worried about what he was going to say when he got to Kayra's house—if she was home. And Malik, he wanted to stay clear of any gun shots there might be once Kayra saw Jake.

Chapter 10

Kayra rushed home to check her mailbox to see if anyone had written her, but there was only a utility bill and a letter from her mother. Kayra clutched her two pieces of mail tightly in her hands and ran to her apartment to escape the cold, fourteen-degree temperature, which was relatively mild for Chicago in January. Once inside, she yelled "HOME, SWEET HOME!" She looked at her messy apartment and decided that cleaning would be the perfect therapy to take her mind off things.

Kayra quickly undressed and searched the dresser drawers for some shabby clothes to put on. After two or three sets of warm-ups and tennis shoes, she finally decided on a University of Houston sweatshirt and an old pair of denim jean shorts, which showed most of her round butt cheeks. She found a red scarf and tied it around her head. "Ready for work! Let me start in the bathrooms, I'm sure they're filthy enough." She grabbed some cleaning supplies, put on a pair of rubber gloves and started scrubbing the toilets. Before she could get started, the doorbell rang. "Damn, who can that be? I knew this would happen as soon as I got started. That's why this place looks the way it does!" She stood from the toilet with the scrub brush still in her hand and moved towards the door.

Malik and Jake were outside—both nervous as hell. Malik stayed in the car and was scrunched down in the front seat trying not to be seen, while Jake stood at the front door rehearsing what he was going to say. He rang the doorbell one more time.

"I'm coming!" shouted Kayra. Without thinking she opened the door. There stood Jake, tall, dark and handsome. Kayra was in utter shock with her mouth wide open and the pink toilet brush still in her hand.

"What the hell are you doing here?" asked Kayra as calm as she could because she was still kinda glad to see him. "I told you I never wanted to see you again!" Kayra was just about ready to slam the door, when Jake spoke up and pleaded for her forgiveness.

"Kayra, please, please listen to me. I know how you must feel. I was wrong," confessed Jake.

"You know how I feel?" Kayra raised the toilet brush and faked like she was going to swing it. "I should show you how I feel alright!" She took a swing at Jake's head with the toilet bowl brush (missing, of course). Malik saw what was going on from the car. "Whoop! There she goes! I tried to tell him."

"Wait a minute, let me finish!" yelled Jake as he jumped back, scared to death that Kayra was going to pop him. "I'm sorry about what I did. I do really care about you, and I promise nothing like this will ever happen again. That stuff at the club, was all just a big misunderstanding. That girl was somebody I'd just met. I'll admit, she was getting a little too friendly. Kayra waved the brush again.

"She was getting a little too friendly, huh? You must think I'm a damn fool! I saw you and her all hugged up. I even saw you kissing her! So no, don't come to my house with all these damn lies and expect me to believe them and just pretend everything is okay.

It's not! I thought when I met you, you'd be different than all the rest. I really was willing to give you a chance, despite my better judgment. I've been through this kind of pain before—yes, I said pain because you really hurt me.

Kayra dropped the brush on the floor and started crying. Jake walked closer and tried to hold her. Kayra snatched away.

"Not anymore Jake! You won't do this to me again! I've found somebody who truly cares about me and who's not going to play these games. Now go, and don't come back!"

"But, Kayra!" replied Jake as he reached for her.

Kayra slammed the door in his face.

"I'll call the police next time!" she yelled through the door. Jake stood leaned against the other side of the door and stared at it as if he was expecting it to open. There was no such luck. Malik raised up and got out of the car.

"Come on man, it's over!" Jake turned around with tears running down his cheeks and walked slowly to the car.

Kayra slid down the door and sat on the floor crying. When she was done, her spirit felt better about the decision to be with Pam. She wasn't completely comfortable with the relationship yet, but she figured it would have to be better than what she had already gone through. At least Pam had been a part of her life longer than any man—they went in and out of her life like revolving doors. Kayra stopped crying, stood up, picked up the toilet brush, and continued cleaning.

Malik tried to console Jake.

"Don't let it get you down. You were wrong, but you tried to straighten things out. Kayra made her decision, you just gotta live with it."

"I can't!"

"You got to! You can't make her accept your apology!"

"I fucked up, huh?"

"Yeah, you did! Now let's go!"

Jake and Malik got back in the car and headed for Malik's house. When they got there, Malik asked Jake to come inside and relax.

"We might as well watch this damn movie, it's been here for three days and I ain't seen the ending yet! Everytime it started getting good I ended up falling asleep. Sometimes it ain't even worth renting movies. You may as well just buy it. That way you can keep it for as long as you want and not have to worry about the cost. That shit adds up!"

Jake agreed and pretended he was interested in the movie. He was really preoccupied with thoughts of Kayra and what his next move should be to get her back. Malik looked at his face and told him, "Forget about it!" By the time the movie was over, Jake had decided the best thing to do was to just stay on the "down low". After she'd calmed down, surely she would let him at least call her. Then Jake remembered something Kayra said, about having somebody else, and it pissed him off!

"Who could it be?" Jake wondered. "Malik, did I tell you she said she had somebody else?"

"What are you talking about?"

"Kayra. She said she was dating somebody else now."

"Oh, she did? That was quick, who is he?"

"I don't know, but I am going to find out! She couldn't have found somebody new that quick. It must be somebody she used to kick it with and now she has run back to him."

"Man, leave that shit alone! Let's say you did find out who he was, what did you plan on doing? You ain't doing nothing but asking for trouble. See, your feelings are hurt now. That's what the real deal is. She let you know you ain't the only one for her. You have a bruised ego, my brother."

"Are you blaming me for all this? It seems to me like I'm the one who got played!"

"Where are you going?" asked Malik.

"Home!" snapped Jake.

Malik knew Jake was up to something. He figured he'd done all he could to talk some sense into him. "See ya my brother, you're on your own!" said Malik. Jake didn't say a word and slammed the door. He decided next weekend he would stake out Kayra's apartment to finally see her mystery man.

Chapter 11

After Jake had gone out the door, Kayra finished the cleaning and sat on her white leather couch to admire the hard work she did.

"Nice and clean, just the way I like it! And it smells sensational —'Pine Sol' fresh! She grabbed a book from the coffee table and read the title, *Understanding the Black Man*. "I understand them alright! I understand their asses ain't no good!" Kayra slammed the book down on the table, and knew immediately why she'd put off reading it in the first place. "I feel dirty. I need a bath." After smelling under her arms, Kayra went into the bathroom and ran a steaming hot bath with the usual drops of strawberry bath beads.

As the tub filled up, Kayra hurried to take off her smelly clothes. She relaxed in the bubbling water and thought about what had taken place with Pam. The encounter both frightened and tantalized her. For a brief moment she imagined Pam's hands caressing her body. The image made Kayra horny and she began touching herself. The motion of her fingers inside her kitten got faster and faster as she got wetter and wetter until she almost worked herself to an explosive orgasm. Kayra tried to stay in control, but she laid in the tub unable to contend with her hidden passions. Her body kept throbbing and vibrating until she began to work up a sweat and became breathless. She put her hand back between her legs and started moving up and down stroking her swollen clitoris. Before she knew it, she was screaming and moaning as she felt the warm tingle rush down her body.

When Kayra came, she shouted out Pam's name; afterwards, she found herself too exhausted to finish bathing. Instead, she just washed up in all the necessary places and got out of the tub. Then she sat naked on the bed and thought about what she had done. *"This is crazy, what am I doing? I can't keep this up. I don't know who I am anymore! I've turned into some kind of freak who fucks herself and other women. All I wanted was a good man in my life. That's all! As much as I find myself attracted to Pam, I don't know if being with a woman is the right thing for me. Maybe it is!"* Kayra walked and shook her head in disgust. *"I don't know if I am in love or lust. And what about Jake? Maybe I was too hard on him. It doesn't matter because after today, he might not ever want to talk to me again anyway. I'm so confused!"*

Kayra fell on the bed and covered her face with a pillow. She took a short nap to try to escape the taunting thoughts she had. When she woke up she decided to call Pam. Things felt so different between them now and awkward, but she called anyway.

"Hello," answered Pam.

"Hi, Pam, how are you?" asked Kayra while nervously twisting her hair.

"What's up Kayra, I didn't think you were going to call."

"To be honest, I didn't think I was either."

"I'm glad you did! What have you been doing with yourself since you left?"

"Not too much. I finally cleaned my dirty apartment. When I finished, I took a nice hot bubble bath to soothe my nerves."

"A bath, huh?" asked Pam with a sexy tone in her voice.

"Yes, a bath" replied Kayra trying to ignore Pam's flirting.

"Was it any fun without me?"

Kayra didn't answer because she knew she had masturbated for the first time in her life thinking of none other than the inquirer. It felt so good! Should she tell Pam what she did or would it be better to keep it to herself for now? Pam, impatiently, asked Kayra again for an answer.

"Well, was it?"

Kayra bucked in silence for just a brief moment. "No, it was just a bath—nothing special."

Pam knew Kayra was lying, but she didn't push the issue. She realized Kayra might have felt uneasy if she did.

"I'm sorry to hear that. I thought it might have reminded you of me! Anyway, what are you doing the rest of the day?"

"Girl, I think I'm gonna stay here at home and get my things ready for work tomorrow," laughed Kayra trying to play Pam's comment off.

"I heard that. I need to be doing the same," said Pam. Out of curiosity, she decided to ask Kayra one more question. "Have you heard from Jake?"

"Hell, yes!" answered Kayra quickly. "As a matter of fact, he had the nerve to come over here!"

"I knew it!" yelled Pam. "What the hell is he doing coming over there to see you? He has no business trying to come back into your life after what he did to you!"

"I know. When he was here, I told his ass exactly how I felt about him and what he did. You don't have to worry, after what I told him, he won't be back. I'm sure of it!" insisted Kayra.

"Well, I hope you're right!" said Pam trying to calm down. "If he keeps this up, I'll have to tell him myself to stay away."

"That won't be necessary." assured Kayra. "I got to go now, Pam. I'll give you a call later this week."

"That's fine, maybe we can do lunch one day," replied Pam.

Pam felt a little disappointed by her conversation with Kayra. She wanted to know how she felt about her because she was afraid Kayra might have changed her mind about having an intimate relationship.

When she got off the phone, Pam went into the kitchen and poured herself a glass of wine. She took a few sips and got angry at the mere thought of Jake trying to come between her and Kayra.

She wondered, if there was anything she could do, to make sure Jake wouldn't be the one to keep her and Kayra apart. *"What can I do?"* she thought. Pam took another sip from the glass. "Maybe I should forget the whole thing. We could just chalk it up as a one-night-stand and let time patch things up." Pam finished her drink, started to pour another, and realized that she was getting a little tipsy. "I'd better not," she said while putting her glass in the sink. "I'm not going to let Jake's slick ass worry me. He will get his and I'll make sure of that!"

At home, Kayra went to bed and tried not to concern herself with Pam or Jake. She'd resisted Pam's temptation, and she hadn't heard from Jake again.

Chapter 12

*I*t was Monday and Jake looked forward to going to his office today. He thought it would help him to forget about his horrible weekend. He was restless most of the night devising a plan to get Kayra back, even though she was preoccupied (all of a sudden) with some other man out of the blue. "I can't think about that shit now, I got to make some money!"

Jake strutted to his closet and decked himself out in one of his designer suits from Italy. He rushed to Alexander's, his men's store located in the exclusive Oak Street shopping district in Downtown Chicago. On Jake's agenda for the day were five interviews. All of them with women applying for his assistant manager's position and he was not in the mood to deal with them. The last thing he wanted to do was sit and listen to a bunch of women.

When Jake got to the office, his store manager Sydney was already there to greet him.

"Well, good morning, Mr. Alexander."

"Hi, Sydney. How are you today?"

"Fine, Sir. How was your weekend?"

"You don't want to know!" answered Jake as he trotted up the spiral staircase leading to his office. As soon as he opened the door and turned on the light, he noticed his answering machine was blinking. "Hmmm, I wonder who called so early? Maybe it was Kayra," he thought as he rushed to the phone. He pressed the button and eagerly listened to the message.

"Jake, good morning. This is Yolanda. I didn't hear from you last night, so I wanted to make sure everything was alright. I'll be at work all day so call me there. In fact, let's do lunch," continued Yolanda.

"Damn! I swear, that girl must be whipped!" said Jake laughing and not wanting to be bothered with her. "I gotta be more careful; sometimes I don't know how good I am! Why couldn't that have been Kayra calling to say how much she loved me and needed me to make love to her all night long. Yeah, right! Wishful thinking I guess," said Jake as he stood from his desk and looked out his window.

His first applicant made her way in at about 9:00 a.m. By the time he got through with the fourth at four o'clock, he was exhausted—at least until Regina Jackson walked in, his last applicant. She was a voluptuous and sexy woman from East Orange, New Jersey who had just moved to Chicago. When she stood in the doorway, Jake's body shivered with excitement. Surprisingly the day, which started out as long and drawn-out, suddenly came to life with Jake's now erected penis doing the same.

He greeted Regina and immediately started his patented charm, which had kept him in woman trouble most of his life. But he soon realized what he was doing and tried to catch himself before things got out of hand.

"I'm thinking with the wrong head!" he said to himself. Then he began to try hard to keep the interview strictly professional. However, after a while he found himself still trying to rap to her, not to mention he was also staring at her large breasts.

By the time Jake finally got through the interview, he knew he wanted Regina for the job. But to be politically correct, he didn't offer the position to her on the spot. As Regina left, Jake complimented her on how well organized her resume was and told her that she would be contacted if she got the job. Before she left, Jake couldn't help but to flirt with her once more.

"Ms. Jackson, or may I call you Regina?"

"Regina's fine," she quickly answered with a big smile.

"Well, Regina, off the record let me please say, you have the loveliest eyes and the prettiest smile I have ever seen!"

Regina's face turned red as she blushed and smiled again showing her pearly white teeth.

"Thank you."

"I just had to tell you that. I hope you don't mind. I really look forward to seeing you again," said Jake. As he opened the door he looked into Regina's eyes, winked, and gave her a big smile. She left his office, and headed back down the spiral stairs. Jake closed the door, returned to his desk, and thought about what he'd just done.

"I don't know what's getting into me. I got enough problems with women, for me to be pulling this kinda of shit! But damn, she's fine!" yelled Jake out loud. "I guess I'm like the male version of Zora in Spike Lee's movie, "*She's Gotta Have It.*" He should cast me in the movie and call it *"He's Gotta Have It."* I bet all the brothers would relate to that! It probably would be Spike's best box office hit."

Now on the other hand, Malik didn't need another woman in his life. He needed a job! It just so happened Nicole worked in the human relations department at North Star Financial Company. She scheduled Malik to come apply for a position. He went into the office and checked the openings posted on the board. Malik found a position in the accounting department as a bookkeeper, which was something he always wanted to do. He filled out the paperwork and Nicole called him in for the interview.

It was awkward at first for both of them because they could not keep from gazing into each other's eyes.

Even though they both knew he had the job, they had to go through the formalities.

After the interview, Nicole offered Malik the job, which he accepted with a big smile on his face. Nicole was glad she was able to help him and see him so happy.

"Thank you very much, Ms. Anderson," said Malik with a wink.

"You're quite welcome," replied Nicole with a big smile of her own.

"Will I see you later?" asked Malik.

"Sure!" answered Nicole.

♥

Malik was ecstatic. Later that evening, he rushed over to Jake's house to tell him the good news. He ran up to the door as fast as he could to see if Jake was there.

"Hey Jake, open up!" yelled Malik as he continued knocking on the door.

Jake slowly made it to the door to answer Malik's cry. He was still fully dressed because he had been too tired to change clothes. Jake shouted through the door at Malik, wondering what all the excitement was all about.

"What's up! Are you trying to bust the door down?"

He opened the door and Malik did his usual routine of running and jumping on Jake's favorite chair, the black leather recliner he had gotten from Indigo as an anniversary gift. Jake smiled and closed the door. He went into the den, where Malik began telling him what happened. He sat on the couch and ignored the seating arrangement.

"Man, guess what happened to me today," said Malik.

"Look, I don't feel like playing guessing games tonight. Just tell me what's up! Hold on. Hold on! Just for kicks, let's see—you hit the lotto!"

"No!" Malik quickly answered.

"You mean you didn't hit the *fantasy five* or some shit like that?"

"No!"

"Let me see, you got a promotion on your job. *Oops, I forgot, you ain't got no job man!*" said Jake jokingly as he cried laughing. "That's alright, you're still my boy and all that! I'm gonna start calling you Tommy—from the 'Martin' show." Both Malik and Jake laughed.

"Not anymore!" said Malik who'd stopped laughing and now had a straight look on his face.

"Not anymore what?" asked Jake as he stopped laughing too.

"I got a job now!" Malik announced proudly again.

Jake moved to the edge of the couch looking very surprised.

"You got a job?"

"You heard me. That's what I came over here to tell you. I got a J-O-B! *So what's up dogg!*" joked Malik imitating Tommy from "Martin."

The two laughed again as Jake stood up and gave Malik a big hug. "So how did this happen?" asked Jake curiously.

"Well, it's like this, Nicole and I were kicking it around last night. We got into this deep discussion on self-esteem and how brothers need to quit making excuses and start getting themselves together. The "Million Man March" was just the beginning. It's time to carry the energy from there and use it to make a light shine in your own life. After that, I broke down and told her all the shit I'm going through, especially how hard it's been for me to find a job. Nicole understood exactly where my head was.

"Yeah, she knew where your head was—probably between her legs! That's what she understood!" interrupted Jake.

"Man I'm for real!" said Malik while trying to keep from laughing. "But she did understand. I went this morning and filled out an application. She interviewed me and hired me right on the spot."

"That's good man, I'm happy for you. I'm glad you're getting yourself together and everything is working out for you. I tried offering you a job a long time ago but you were trippin'. You kept talking about clothes wasn't your thing and you wouldn't fit in if you worked in one of my stores. I guess you didn't want to work for me."

"No my brother. It wasn't like that. I just didn't want to feel like a charity case or something."

"How can you say some bullshit like that! We've been partners too long. It's about taking care of one another because there are only two times you should look down on another brother. One, is when he's dead and laid to rest. The second, is when you're helping him up! So don't give me that shit. It's your own fault if you let your ego and pride stop you from letting me help you. Besides, I wouldn't be giving you a handout, only a job. You still would have to work if you expected to get paid! So how is that charity?"

"Alright, you made your point!" screamed Malik holding his head. The two gave each other a "high five" as Jake changed the subject and began to tell Malik about the interviews he had conducted and how fine Regina was.

"Man, I had five interviews today and all of them were women. You know after the weekend I had, I wasn't up to talking to a bunch of females. But it really wasn't so bad. Let me tell you about the last one. She's got it going on and on and on! She looked just like an Amazon Princess. Tall, bronzed, long shining black hair that went down her back. Her body, just heavenly!"

"Dude, I don't know what I'm going to do about you and these damn women! I told you. You need help!"

As Jake loosened his tie, he decided it was time to get on Malik about sitting in his chair.

"Yeah my brother, can you get your ass up so I can have my chair back? Every man should have a chair in the house he calls his own. And that one you're always sitting in is mine. So, see ya!"

"I didn't know it was so dear to you. I'm outta here! I'll check with you tomorrow." laughed Malik.

"Peace." Jake answered and shut the door. "I think I'm going to take this suit off and take me a nice hot bath. Then I'll take a little nap and I should be ready to make a few phone calls." Jake walked to the window and saw Malik still outside. Then he raised it to speak.

"Is everything okay?"

"I'm just thinking. Go back inside!"

"Cool. I got some calls to make anyway."

"I bet you do. You're probably going to call your new *Amazon* dream girl and give her a job so your hot ass can have a toy to play with at your office. You better be careful. One day you might decide you want to "get your freak on" and you end up in court for sexual harassment—since you'll be her boss. Oh, by the way, I didn't forget that we were supposed to go to church.

"Okay, Malik. I promise I'll make it this Sunday. Now, go ahead and get outta here so I can get me some sleep." Jake closed the door and took off all his clothes, right down to his silk boxers. He left them in the center of the living room floor and then ran and did a belly flop into the bed. "Oh, it sure feels good to lay down!" He rolled around a few minutes until he found the right spot. He stopped and fell off to sleep before he had time to think about taking a bath.

♥

Malik made it back home to his apartment. He hurried inside to check his answering machine, hoping that Nicole had called him. She hadn't. His only call was from the landlord who was hounding him again about paying the rent due on Friday.

"I told his ass he don't have to worry. I guess he's trippin' because I've been late the past couple of months. Anyway, let me get off that shit. I got a job now and everything is gonna' be all good! It might take me a minute or two to get caught up on all these bills—I'll be straight by the summer."

Chapter 13

Kayra was hard at work teaching her 12th grade class at Belmont High, located on the Northside of town. Normally, she would have taught a grade-school class like the 4th grade, but for some reason the school had trouble keeping high school teachers. When Belmont called Kayra and offered her a position, the first question they asked was if she was willing to take on the challenge of teaching the high school kids. Since Kayra didn't have a job at the time, it wasn't a hard choice to make. She was more than happy to accept the job. She had been out of work for the past few months. Every school in the districts she had applied had turned her down because of funding cuts. Today was her second week assigned at Belmont, but her first day in the classroom. The previous week was spent at the Board of Education in processing.

As the bell rang, Kayra walked into the classroom and what she saw made her want to turn around. The students were literally out of control. Two boys were teasing a girl, who had exceptionally large breasts for her age, while another one stood behind her trying to feel them. Other kids were in the back of the room smoking cigarettes. Another kid was standing on his desk cursing at two girls over nothing. A young brother with dark shades on looked like he was smoking a joint until he heard the door open and tried to throw it out of the window. Kayra still recognized the familiar smell it left lingering in the air. Balls of paper flew across the room like showers of snow.

After her initial shock, Kayra finally got the nerve up to go to her desk. The students ignored her presence and kept doing whatever they were doing. She set her briefcase on the desk and gazed over the classroom with a look of *why am I here?* Suddenly, the thought of the weekend passed through her mind. She had flashbacks of Jake and Yolanda at the club. He lied to her as if she was stupid and got her hopes up only to break her heart. A rage rose up in Kayra and before she knew it she had gone into a frenzy as she watched the crazy ass kids do their thing.

"Shut up and sit down right now!" shouted Kayra as loud as she could. The kids looked and saw her furious expression and flaming red eyes, which could have set a house on fire.

Instantly, all the conversations stopped and everyone quietly started making their way to their seats. "You two boys over there!" pointed Kayra at the boys with the girl who had the big breasts. You had better come over here and leave her alone before I come over there and snatch your damn heads off your shoulders!" The two boys stopped and ran to their seats so fast you could feel the breeze as they went by.

"If I ever see either one of you doing that again, be assured I will have both your asses arrested and put under the jail! You folks smoking, put those cigarettes out! This is not a pool hall. This is a classroom and from now on you will treat it as such."

"I don't know what's been going on in here but it's going to change starting today! I've had a bad weekend and I'm not up for having a bad week, so you'd better listen to what I'm saying. Otherwise, we're going to have a hard time getting along, and trust me, you don't want to get on my bad side these days! You kids are not some animals in a cage, so stop acting like you are. You are students who should be in this classroom trying to learn. My job as a teacher is to help you learn. Your job is to behave like students so you can make my job easier. Do you understand me?"

"Yeah." mumbled the kids.

"Alright, that's enough. Just one collective "yes!" will do just fine for an answer," said Kayra as she started to calm down.

"Yes!" replied the kids loudly in unison.

"Now, let's get the rules of this classroom straight. There will be no cussing, smoking, throwing, fighting, touching and no name-calling. You will show me, and each other respect. You will come to class prepared by bringing your textbooks, notebook paper and your pencils and pens. I expect all the homework I assign to be done and completed on time. If you need help with any assignments let me know. I understand that since you're seniors all of you think you're grown, but you're not! I'm the only adult in this classroom, so remember that. Do we understand each other?"

Without waiting for an answer, Kayra began her lesson as the students quietly pulled out their notebooks and listened for further instructions. When the day ended, Kayra felt a great sense of accomplishment, although she was still trying to get over the shock of how the day had begun.

She had heard rumors of how wild the kids were at Belmont, but she thought it was only because the school had all black students and was located in an all black community. During her week processing time at the Board of Education office, she had only visited the school once before she started and nothing she saw gave her any indication things would be so crazy. "Where is Joe Clark when you need him?" laughed Kayra.

She decided she would either have to put up with them and attempt to make some sort of difference, or head back to Houston as quickly as she could. She chose to stay. That evening, she packed up her briefcase and made her way home. While driving, Kayra wondered what Pam was doing and how her day had gone since she hadn't called her all day.

♥

Pam had her mind on Kayra as well. All day at her office she considered calling Kayra, even though today was one of her most productive days in awhile. She met with one of her clients, an author who had published his first novel and was looking for exposure.

While meeting with him, in walked Larry Contrell, a big Hollywood movie star who, as it turns out, spends most of his time in Chicago when he's not acting. He had heard about Pam's work when she was living in California and decided he was interested in her possibly representing him. When Pam saw Mr. Contrell, she rushed the author out the door and told him, "I'll get back with you soon!" Then she ran and greeted the big star. The other two assistants of Pam's stopped what they were doing to watch Mr. Contrell as he stood in the lobby waiting for Pam.

"Hi, Mr. Contrell," said Pam with a big smile.

"Hello to you too Ms. Johnson. It's a pleasure to meet you."

"It is?" replied Pam surprised he even knew she existed.

"Sure is," answered Contrell with a warm smile. "I heard a lot about you from the program you put together for a guy who was a co-star of mine a few years ago. Because of what you did for him, he now has his own TV show, which is why I'm here. I've enjoyed tremendous success and I want somebody on my team who knows how to keep that happening for me. And frankly Ms. Johnson, I believe you are that person."

"Well, I really don't know what to say. I'm a big fan of yours and I would love the opportunity to be apart of your continued success. How long are you going to be in town?" replied Pam smiling.

"I'll be leaving tomorrow evening. I have to be at the studio for a late night shoot. But I'm free the rest of the evening."

"Maybe I can spend some time with you today, to get an idea of the type of public relations program you feel will suit your needs. I also would like to get to know more about you so I'll be able to offer you ideas based on what type of person you really are."

Mr. Contrell extended his hand to Pam to seal the deal.

"Sounds like a wonderful idea Pam. I have to make a quick visit to a friend, but I'll be back a little later to get started."

"I look forward to your return," replied Pam very confidently.

Pam escorted Mr. Contrell to the office door. When he exited, she turned around to her staff and screamed, "*yes!*" as she jumped up in the air. Pam ran to all of her people and gave them a big hug and a "high five." It was the first time she had gotten a client with the renown popularity and celebrity status of Larry Contrell. Pam went back into her office, got her purse and keys, then drove straight to her house. She took a quick bath, changed clothes and drove back to the office. When she got there everyone had left for the day. Pam waited patiently, while she thought of questions she wanted and needed to ask.

♥

Mr. Contrell made his way back and he and Pam had their meeting. Afterwards, she returned home more excited than ever about the big contract. She still thought to herself, however, *"I haven't talked to Kayra in two days, maybe I should call her."* Instead she decided against making the call because she started to feel too guilty.

It turns out Pam and Mr. Contrell, or Larry as Pam now refers to him, instead of calling it a night after their meeting had gone into Pam's office and had a little "69" action going on top of her cherry oak desk. Apparently, during the course of the night, they got the hots for each other and before they knew it, things got out of control.

Now Pam had a hard time dealing with her feelings about what had happened. She knew with Larry it was only a physical attraction, but it was the same shit Jake did to Kayra. After all, what good is it to love someone if your actions don't show it? Pam realized that and it seemed everybody, including herself, was fucking Kayra around. "What am I going to do? I guess the only thing I can do is forget about this and pretend it never happened!"

Pam knew Kayra didn't know that she had lied to her about not ever being with a woman before, nor had she revealed some other unflattering things in her past. But in the end, Pam felt everything would work itself out and she undressed and crawled into bed. She laid quietly and thought it was kinda nice to know that her affections for Kayra hadn't made her lose all her attraction to men. "They're dogs, but they can still be used for something! Hell, they do it to us all the time! And, 'Hello,' I do like a little dick—every now and then!"

♥

Kayra felt things couldn't continue as they were. She decided to call Pam and suggest they have a face to face meeting to come to a workable solution. Kayra made the call.

"Pam I've been thinking. You know how I feel about you and our friendship. I have to be honest, things between us have been awkward. I really don't know how to be comfortable with our friendship anymore. We need to get together, maybe this weekend. We can talk face to face. I love you and I don't want to lose our friendship. It would just kill me if that was to happen."

"You're right Kayra, let's get together to talk." The two agreed to meet at Pam's house on Friday night at ten o'clock. Hopefully before the night was over, they would reach an understanding.

Chapter 14

*J*ake must find out who Kayra's new love interest is. Or who he thinks it is.

"This weekend I'm going to follow her ass and maybe she will meet with him. I'll be there to catch their asses! I'll break her fuckin' neck and then his! Jake realized what he was saying and tried to calm himself down. "I ain't going to do all that, but I still feel that bitch gave me a raw deal, too!"

♥

The week flew by and Friday night came. Kayra arrived at Pam's house at about 9:50p.m. As she pulled into the driveway, Jake, who had been trailing her, parked at the corner. He slowly stopped the car and turned off his headlights. He watched Kayra quickly get out of her car and walk toward the front door. As Kayra got closer, she noticed Pam's back gate was open. The only light on in the house was a small nightlight that shined through the bathroom window. Suspicious, Kayra decided to go around to the back door to check things out. "She probably won't hear me knocking but I'll try anyway. Maybe, I'll scare her like she does me all the time!" Just as she got inside the gate, Kayra heard the low muffled sound of music playing. The sound seemed to relax Kayra a little bit as she crept around through the dark shadows of the yard. The "Hawk", with it's howling winds pushed her back one step for every two she took forward.

Only a block away, Jake sat angrily in the car as he mumbled to himself. "This must be the stud's house Kayra left me for. Look at her walking like she owns the damn place. I can't take this shit anymore! I'm going in too!"

Kayra finally made her way to Pam's back door. She walked up and knocked on it as hard as she could. No one answered. Just as she lifted her fist to knock again, she heard a loud noise in the bushes. Suddenly, a large cat jumped out the brushes and landed on Kayra's shoulder. It started clawing at her eyes. Frantically, Kayra tried to shake it off her. "Stop! Stop!" she yelled. She finally got a good grip on the beast and tried to pull it off her as she ran around screaming.

Jake got out of his car and went to Pam's front door. He wanted to confront the man who had taken Kayra and given him little or no chance to get her back. He banged on the door. When no one answered, Jake angrily lifted his muscular leg and kicked in the door. It collapsed on its hinges instantly.

Meanwhile, poor Kayra had just ended her bout with the cat. When all was said and done, the cat had left her alone, but not before being clubbed on the head several times with a thick branch Kayra picked up to defend herself. With all the wrestling, Kayra ended up standing in Pam's neighbor's yard crying and bleeding from the large scratches left by the wild cat.

Jake rushed inside to check the house and yelled for Kayra to come out. "Kayra, I want to talk to you. I know you're in here. Where are you?" he inquired loudly.

Then he went to the back of the large condominium, looked in each of the first two bedrooms and found them empty.

Kayra stopped crying and had regained her composure. She went back up to the door and gave it a big hard bang and yelled, "Pam!" Just as she did, the unlocked door flew open from a big gust of wind. Kayra slowly went inside. "Pam where are you?" whispered Kayra very quietly. The music was still playing as Kayra made her way towards the sound. "Okay, where is Pam and where is that damn radio so I can shut it off!"

Jake came to the last bedroom in the house, which is also where the music was coming from. The door to the bedroom was closed. Jake knocked on it and shouted, "Kayra, are you in there?" When he didn't get an answer, he turned the doorknob this time, before he tried to kick the door down. Luckily for the door it was open. Jake was also glad he didn't have to do his *Rambo* routine again, like he used to get inside the house. Slowly, he opened the door and went inside the bedroom. He noticed clothes thrown on the floor and broken furniture everywhere. "What the hell happened here?" Jake ignored the loud blaring music from a speaker laying on the floor and kept walking around in confusion. He went into the large bathroom, located in the corner of the huge bedroom. When he entered he almost went into shock. He saw a woman's naked body laying on the floor, completely covered in blood. "Oh no! Oh no!" shouted Jake. He turned his head to keep from throwing up.

When his stomach settled, he eased to the mangled body and just as he reached to check her pulse, Kayra walked into the room. She saw Jake bending over the body and screamed.

"Oh my God, Pam! Jake, what have you done? What did you do to her? God! Oh God!"

Jake stood up from the body and Kayra saw all the blood and screamed again. She tried to run out the bathroom but Jake jumped and grabbed her by the arm.

"Stop Kayra! Wait a minute."

Kayra turned to face Jake with tears running down her face as she shook with fear. "I didn't do this Kayra. You gotta believe me!"

Too afraid to listen, Kayra screamed, "Let me go! Let me go damn it!" She snatched her arm from Jake's hand and ran out the house, pulling down everything she could. She slammed doors trying to stop Jake from chasing her. Jake ran behind her still trying to explain. Kayra finally got outside and rushed to her car.

Jake stopped at the doorway realizing that it was too late to try and convince Kayra of his innocence. "It's time to get the hell outta here before the cops come and take my ass off to jail!" Jake watched as Kayra jumped in her car and sped away. Then he ran back inside to the bathroom and looked around for anything that might have shown he'd been there.

Afterwards, he took a towel from the shower and went through the house wiping everything to remove his fingerprints off whatever he might have touched. He finished and ran out the back door to his car parked at the corner. He sped off and drove about a half a mile down the street, before he heard the distant sounds of sirens blaring in the silence of the night. "Oh shit! I guess Kayra must have called the police already! I knew that bitch would sell me out!"

Jake raced home to get some of his things. When he got to his street, he slowed down and eased around the corner to make sure no police had gotten to his house before him. All was quiet for now, no sirens and no lights.

♥

When Kayra got to her driveway, she thought it would be best if she disappeared for awhile just in case Jake tried to come after her. She parked her car and ran as fast as she could to her house, leaving the car door wide open. Nervously, she opened her front door, stepped inside and slammed it behind her. She locked every lock she could. Then she collapsed on the floor.

"How could this happen! Pam never did anything to anybody. Why God, did you let this happen?

I loved her! She was the only sister I knew. My one true friend and lover!" Kayra cried for over an hour before she finished and wiped the tears from her eyes. Later, Kayra felt a sense of calm and peace about the whole situation. Instead of trembling through the house like a maniac, she coolly started packing some clothes. Still exhausted, she got sleepy and before she knew it, she had fallen asleep.

As Kayra rested peacefully at home, Jake made his way to Malik's house. He knocked on the door as hard as he could.

"Malik," he shouted. "Malik, open the door now! Open this damn door!"

"What the...." mumbled Malik. Before he could finish Jake pushed the door open and ran inside.

"You have got to help me!"

"What the hell are you talking about! What's wrong? Take your time and tell me what is going on."

"Okay, but I don't have much time! I decided I was going to follow Kayra to find out who she was dating. I stayed out in front of her place tonight until she came out. Then I followed her to a house. The way I figured, it was where her boyfriend lived. I waited for a little while, then I got mad and decided to confront both of them and tell Kayra I wanted her back. I went to the door, nobody answered, so I let myself in."

"What do you mean, let yourself in?" interrupted Malik. "Was the door open or something?"

"Yeah or something!" replied Jake. "For some reason it opened when I kicked it!"

"You did what?"

Jake ignored Malik and continued explaining.

"When I got inside, I didn't see Kayra or the guy. I heard the radio playing and followed the music into the bedroom where it was coming from. I looked in the bathroom and that's when I found her!"

"Found who? Kayra?" asked Malik confused.

"No. It was a dead woman! I don't know who she was because she was all cut up and covered in blood."

"What!" shouted Malik. "Did you call the police?"

"No, let me finish. As I was bending over to see if I could help her, in walked Kayra. She saw me and freaked out!"

"What? She thought you killed her?"

"You damn right!" shouted Jake. "And she wouldn't listen to nothing I had to say. She ran out the house like she was scared I was going to kill her."

"Can you blame her?"

"Anyway, man what the hell am I going to do? When I left my house to come over here, I heard the police coming for my ass."

Malik looked like he was going to panic. He paced the floor and picked up the phone and then hung it right back up.

"I know they're going to eventually come here looking for you. I don't want you to go to jail. What are we gonna do?" whined Malik, as he nervously picked up the phone and hung it up...picked up the phone and hung it up...picked up the phone and hung it up. "You got to go, Jake."

Jake saw Malik about to lose it.

"Calm down man." He stood up, grabbed Malik by the arm and led him to the couch to sit down. "Do like me; close your eyes and take deep breaths. See, watch me. Inhale and slowly exhale." Malik watched and then tried. He inhaled and exhaled slowly. After a minute or two, Jake stopped. "Do you feel better now?"

"Yeah, but what are we gonna do?" He picked up the phone and hung it up again.

"I don't know what we're going to do but you need to quit that fucking shit you're doing with the phone!" shouted Jake, totally irritated.

"Okay!" replied Malik. "Let me think, I know where you can go, if she lets you."

"Where?"

"Indigo's house in New York."

"Man, you're crazy!" shouted Jake. "Indigo is not going to let me stay with her."

"Look, you're Railey's father and Indigo is not going to want to see you locked up for God knows how long. Especially, for something you didn't do! Go to her very nicely and explain what happened, just like you did with me. If she doesn't say yes, give her some good down home charm. She'll say yes. And I promise you I'll do everything on this end to make sure you get your name cleared."

"Well, maybe you're right. I really don't have much choice, do I? I know it's only a matter of time before they find me here in Chicago. I better go. Give me a call in a couple of days."

"Oh, now you don't mind me fucking with the phone!"

Jake and Malik laughed and shared one last special moment.

♥

While Jake and Malik were busy joking, Kayra's pain was starting to become more bearable. "Thank you Jesus!" she shouted as she watched the muted TV and calmly reflected on what a great friend Pam had been. The memories flew through her mind like a VCR playing the home movies of her life. From time to time she would push the pause button to capture and reflect on a special moment. Tears ran down her face. "That son of a bitch!" yelled Kayra. "How could he do this to me? I could kill his ass for taking her away from me. I hope the police find him and put him away until he rots in hell! Why? Why, did he have to do this to you? He didn't even know about you or about our love affair." Kayra stood up, took a deep breath and tried to exhale the pain away.

Chapter 15

y the time Kayra woke up the next morning, Jake had landed at the airport in New York City.

"*Calling Mr. Jake Alexander. Calling, Mr. Jake Alexander. Please meet your party in the baggage pickup area,*" sounded the friendly voice through the Airport intercom.

"Well, here goes nothing," said Jake to himself and pushed the button in the elevator for the ground floor. During the ride to the bottom level, he thinks what if this is a trick or a setup of some sort. "I know Malik, he won't tell anything he knows to the police. But what if they start pressuring his ass? What am I saying, I know he wouldn't do that!"

The elevator stopped at the baggage pickup area. When the doors opened, Jake immediately saw Indigo and Railey. They stood waiting for his arrival with anticipation. For a moment it reminded him of happier days when they were a family. He still remembers how good it was to have a family and how much in love he and Indigo were. It felt especially good when her face lit up when she saw him. Jake wondered whether the glow would be there this time.

Railey spotted Jake and sure enough, just as he remembered, their faces made him feel right at home. Railey ran to Jake and jumped in his arms.

"Hi, daddy!"

"How are you doing, son? I missed you a lot," said Jake with tears in his eyes.

"I missed you too, daddy."

Jake gave Railey a kiss on the cheek. "I love you!"

"I love you, daddy!"

Indigo smiled as she walked slowly to Jake and wrapped her arms around him. He returned the embrace and just as he relaxed to cherish the moment, Indigo pushed him away. "Now, what is all this about?" she insisted.

"Come on, let's get far away from here and I'll tell you everything. Alright big guy are you ready for daddy to see your house?"

"Sure, daddy. Come on!" Railey jumped out of Jake's arms, grabbed him by the hand, and off they all went to Indigo's car. The entire time they were walking out of the airport and through the parking lot, Jake looked around to make sure no police was coming his way. Every sudden movement or sound made him jump like the fugitive he was. Although he had asked for Indigo's help, the last thing he wanted to do was jeopardize his son seeing him being taken away by the police.

Once inside the car, Jake felt relieved, which made Indigo even more suspicious about what kind of trouble he was in. All Jake had told her when he called was an emergency had came up and he needed a place to stay. She was concerned about her own safety, but more importantly she didn't want to take any chances on Railey getting hurt.

In the past, Jake was known to get himself and others into some pretty strange predicaments. However, nothing seemed quite like this. Indigo had never seen

Jake as afraid as she did now. Whatever it was, she had to know right now!

"Jake, your ass better tell me what you've gotten yourself into, otherwise, I'm taking your ass right back to that damn airport!"

"Okay, you win! I see you are the same old Indigo. You're right, there is something I need to explain to you, but not in front of Railey. You will have to wait until we are alone." Jake took a deep breath and exhaled slowly while his eyes were closed. Indigo kept driving and looked at Jake.

"I don't know what the hell you're so up tight about. I'm the one who's in the dark and on this mystery run with you. Not to mention, I'm worried about having Railey in the middle of all this. I shouldn't be surprised, you're the same old Jake. No matter what, you find a way to piss me off!"

Jake's eyes got big as a car slowed down in front of them. Indigo didn't see it.

"Watch out!" yelled Jake as he tried to grab the steering wheel.

Indigo looked and swerved into the next lane just missing the car.

"Shut up, I saw it!" insisted Indigo.

Railey leaned forward from the back seat and taped Jake on his shoulder.

"Daddy."

"What's up, Railey?"

"Why are you pissing mama off?"

"What boy? Don't let me hear you say that again! Now, sit back and buckle your seat belt."

Indigo smiled as she tried to keep from bursting out laughing.

"What's so funny? I'm glad you find that so amusing!" said Jake angrily.

After that, nobody said a word for the next thirty minutes, until they reached the very posh upscale neighborhood Indigo had recently moved to. They pulled into the driveway of the huge 4,000 sq. ft., three car garage, Mediterranean style home which belonged to Indigo.

Jake raised his eyebrows.

"I guess this is what being one of New York's top advertising agents will get you."

"Only if you're good!" replied Indigo as she parked her white Mercedes 500 SL. She got out the car and gently picked up Railey, who was still asleep. Once inside, she laid him down across his bed, took off his shoes, and put a small blanket over him. Jake watched and before they left the room, he leaned over and gave Railey a big kiss on his forehead and whispered. "I love you."

Jake and Indigo softly said, "Bye-Bye," as they quietly closed the door and went downstairs, where Jake roamed around being nosey.

"Will you please sit your butt down someplace—but don't get too comfortable, I got a feeling you won't be here too long!" said Indigo.

Without saying a word, Jake shook his head and walked into the den where Indigo was sitting on her white, Italian leather couch. She offered him her favorite architecturally designed chair. It was given to her by one of her clients for a successful ad campaign she worked for him. Jake accepted the offer and gently sat down.

"Doesn't that chair fit perfectly?" asked Indigo with a smile on her face. "It's like a man hugging you and gripping your butt at the same time! Ooh, I'm sorry Jake, you wouldn't know about that or would you?" Indigo laughed as Jake, who was still uptight really didn't find Indigo's joking very funny. He just stared glumly ahead. But she didn't care.

"Start talking and tell me what this is all about!" demanded Indigo.

"I really don't know where to begin."

"How about at the beginning!"

"You would say that!"

"Yes I would. Now start talking!"

"Okay, this is the deal. Last week I was supposed to go out with the woman I've been dating for the past four months. Instead, I ended up having this really big fight with Malik and tried to patch things up with him. I suggested he and I go out for a couple of drinks to talk — you know he's like a brother to me. I canceled my date with Kayra, by the way that's her name, and went to the club with Malik. I didn't tell her where I was going, I just said something came up. I know I was wrong for doing it, but I did!"

"Yeah, you're good for that shit!" agreed Indigo impatiently waiting for Jake to get to the real issue.

"Anyway, continued Jake. At the club, we had a couple of drinks and these two women came over. Before we knew it, we were hanging together. During this time, Kayra and Pam were in the club too. We never saw them until they busted Malik and me hugged up with the two women. Kayra and her girlfriend tripped totally out! After that night, Kayra decided she didn't want to see me anymore. The next day I decided to try to straighten things out. She told me that she had started seeing somebody else, so last night I followed her to a house I thought was her boyfriend's. When she went inside, I waited outside for a little while, until I decided to confront them to settle this thing once and for all."

"That's the stupidest thing I ever heard! She already dumped your ass for somebody else. Then you still go follow the woman like that. You got problems!" said Indigo.

Jake disregarded Indigo's comment. "I went to the door, but nobody answered. I went inside and didn't see anybody there either. All I heard was loud music playing and I looked around the house to find where it was coming from. When I got to the bedroom where the music played. It was a mess. Shit was everywhere like somebody had been fighting. I went into the bathroom." Jake hesitated. "I saw a body laying on the floor."

"You saw what?" said Indigo loudly.

"Yes, a dead woman. I won't even go into how she looked. It was horrible! I got closer and saw she had been cut up."

"She was murdered!" yelled Indigo.

"Yeah, but that's not the half of it. I leaned over to look at the body to see if I could help and in walked Kayra. She saw me and accused me of being the murderer."

"She thinks you did it?" shouted Indigo.

"That's exactly what she thinks!" answered Jake. "I tried to explain, but she wouldn't listen. She ran away and called the police. In fact, they were on their way before I even left the house. I don't know how that happened. I guess Kayra must have gotten to a phone real quick. And the rest, well here I am!"

Indigo was now more disgusted than ever with Jake.

"You're telling me you are a fugitive! What the hell is wrong with you? You damn men are always thinking with your dicks! You and I would've still been together, if you hadn't been running the streets chasing every bitch that shook her ass and dressed like a whore in one of those videos! I told you then and I'm telling you now, it's not about how many women you can get, but how well you can take care of the one you have. Make her happy to the best of your ability. Why can't you understand that? It's about making the woman you're with happy and doing the right thing by her. In the long run, all the video babes you're trying to get a little pussy from, ain't gonna be around to help your ass when you need it. If you don't believe me, check the bullshit you're in now. You got yourself all worked up about this Kayra chick or whatever her name is. Now she doesn't even have enough faith in you to believe you didn't kill that woman. That should tell your ass something! She called the police on your ass and who do you come running back to? Me! Ain't this poetic justice. You tell me, what you think I should do after the way you fucked over me and Railey?"

Before Jake could say a word, Indigo continued with her assault.

"Don't answer that! I'll tell you what. I should kick your ass outta my house and outta my life! But I won't do it. Only because of Railey. I don't want him visiting his father behind some cage. It's bad enough you're only able to be a part of his life a few times a year, but at least he knows you're a free man."

"At least for now! That won't last long if you don't help me." replied Jake.

"Help you! What exactly do you want me to do?" asked Indigo.

"All I'm asking is for you to let me stay here a few days until I can figure out a way to find out who really killed that girl."

"How are you prepared to do that? Better yet, how long is it going to take? The longer you stay, the longer I leave myself open to being hauled off to jail right along with your ass. Then who's going to take care of Railey when both of us are locked up?"

"Damn, Indigo. What do you suggest I do? Go to jail for something I didn't do! I'll just be another nigger who's gotten railroaded by the so-called justice system. I think they got enough of us in there and they don't need me!"

Indigo got up and walked around the spacious and beautifully decorated home. She turned and told Jake to follow her. Jake hurriedly obeyed and smiled. He thought his plea for help somehow opened the door for some loving.

"Alright! This is what I'm talking about. Help a brother relieve a little stress! Jake said happily. "And besides, I've missed that sexy ass of yours."

Indigo stopped.

"Right here is where you can think all about this sexy ass of mine and how nice it would feel. That's about as close as you're going to get to it." She opened the door to one of the bedrooms. "This is where you will be staying, at least for one month and then you got to go!"

Jake was relieved Indigo was going to let him stay. The only bad part was, he wouldn't be getting sexed up like he thought he was. His penis had grown large with anticipation, while walking to the bedroom with Indigo.

"Go down big boy. It's a false alarm!"

Indigo laughed and then reminded Jake of the length of his stay.

"You can make jokes all you want to. You only got thirty days. Thirty days, you hear me!"

"Okay, I hear you! Thirty days! I pray I get enough evidence that soon. You know that's not much time at all."

"Yeah, but that's all you got! Better not make yourself too comfortable. I'll see you later."

"It's like that?" asked Jake.

"Exactly like that!" replied Indigo as she turned and went down the hallway to her study.

♥

Later that evening, she peeked her head in Railey's bedroom to see if he had awakened yet.

"Good. He's still sleeping." she whispered. "*I guess I'll leave for a couple of hours, it's a beautiful evening. I need to get out of the house and think about how I'm gonna deal with having Jake back in my life for a whole month.*" thought Indigo. "Jake."

"What?"

"I'm leaving now. Be sure to watch your son, if he wakes up before I get back."

"Okay." replied Jake as Indigo walked to the door and out to her car. When he saw her pull out the drive and out of sight, he felt strange. "Shit. I was hoping I could come here and she would help me figure this crime out. I see I'm on my own with this one, since it's my ass on the line! The first question is, who was she? Next, who might have wanted her dead?"

Jake thought back to the night of the murder. He remembered clearly Kayra shouting something when she walked into the bathroom and saw him. "*I think she called out the name Pam. Pam, that name sounds familiar. I need to get in touch with Malik. No. I'd better wait until a few days to give things time to cool down.*"

Chapter 16

ayra returned to Belmont High with her class. All the students missed her short absence following Pam's death.

"Everybody open your books to chapter nine and start reading," demanded Kayra.

"Why are you doggin' us out?" asked one of the students.

"What do you mean, Sam? Why do you think I'm doggin' you out?"

"Well, you've been trippin' on us all morning. Every time one of us asks a question, you get mad and don't want to talk to us. We heard about your friend getting hurt. We care about you and want you to be your old self again.

"She wasn't hurt, she was killed! How did you hear about what happened anyway? Who told you?"

"Nobody told us, it just got around."

"Forget it! Just read the assignments I gave you. You should keep up with what's going on in class, not my personal life."

Moments later, the classroom door opened and two men surrounded Kayra's desk.

"Are you Kayra Austin?"

"Yes, I am."

"Ms, I'm Detective Robert Hall and this is Detective Kirk Williams. We are here because we need you to come with us so you can answer a few questions."

"But I've already talked to the police. I told them everything I know."

"I'm sure you did, but we still need to find out some specific information. There's been a strange turn of events, since you were last questioned. So please, can we go?"

"What about my class?"

"It's alright, we've already spoken with Mrs. Newsome, the principal. She said she will be sending somebody down right away to take over your class. So, I'm gonna ask you one last time to come with us."

"Okay," said Kayra. She turned around to all the gleaming eyes of the nosey kids staring at her. She waved good-bye. "I want you to do all the questions at the end of chapter nine and turn them in to me tomorrow." The kids started whining like she had just asked them to rewrite the *Constitution of the United States*. "I don't want to hear it!

Kayra and the detectives left the room. "Where do you want to talk?"

"Ms, we're going downtown to the station."

"What! Are you arresting me?" asked Kayra angrily.

"No, not at all. But we can and will, if you don't cooperate," replied one of the detectives.

"Let's go!" replied Kayra.

♥

The short trip to the Chicago Police Department's 12th precinct took only about fifteen minutes, which made Kayra even more nervous. She didn't have time to review in her mind what she had told the police before, and she didn't want to forget something and make herself look guilty. Even though she was telling the truth, she knew if she started giving different versions, the police would find a way to use it against her.

"Please have a seat, Ms. Austin."

"You can call me Kayra."

"Okay, Kayra. Let us go over your statement very quickly. Let's see, on the night of February 2, 1996 at approximately 9:50p.m, you went to 1228 Carol St. to visit your friend—a Ms. Pamela J. Johnson. When you got there, you went to the front door and you didn't get an answer so you went to the back door. Correct?"

Kayra raised her hand off the desk and looked at her manicured fingernails as if she was bored. "Yes that's correct so far."

"When you approached the back door, you said you were attacked by some sort of wild cat."

"That's right, I did!" replied Kayra loudly and with much attitude.

"All this time, you didn't see anyone in or around the house?"

"No, I didn't see anyone."

"After you got the cat off you, you knocked on the door and still got no answer. You noticed the door was ajar, you pushed it opened and went inside. At this time, all you heard was the loud music playing. You looked around and followed the sound into the back bedroom. In the bedroom was a bathroom and in that bathroom, you saw your friend lying on the floor in a pool of blood. And standing over her body was this guy named Jake. When he saw you, he tried to attack you. You screamed and ran out the house. You drove your car to a nearby phone booth and called the police. This you say was about 10:25p.m. Is all this correct?"

"Well, he didn't really attack me. He was more or less trying to explain to me that he didn't kill her. He was trying to keep me from leaving. I told him I didn't want to hear what he had to say and to let me go."

"Did he?"

"Yes, he did. Then I ran to my car and drove off to call the police."

"Ms, I mean Kayra, everything you said is pretty accurate according to what we checked out. But one thing bothered us. When we checked the 911 call, it did show you called at 10:28p.m. However, there were cars already being dispatched at around 10:12p.m.as a result of a tip called into the station. So the question is, who made that call? Do you have any ideas?"

"No," Kayra answered without hesitation.

"Let us help you. First of all, after we did an identification check on the body, we found out that it wasn't your friend Pam! It was a woman named Dee Taylor, who our sources tell us was a friend of Pam."

Kayra almost fell out of her seat in shock.

"Oh my God, where is Pam?" she cried.

"That's what we want to know, too. We think she is the one who made that first call. Did you know Pam kept a diary?"

"No, I didn't."

"In the diary, your friend tells about all of her sexual encounters."

Kayra started moving nervously.

"So what!" she replied. "Is that a crime?"

"No, it's not. We're not just talking about men here, we're talking about women too! Your friend described in some pretty graphic details, her love affairs with these women."

Kayra tried not to look bothered by what the detectives were saying. At the moment, all kinds of things were going through her mind—most of all, Pam was alive! What about all this shit about her and these women? Kayra remembered when she and Pam were together, Pam told her she had never been with a woman before. She said it only happened with her because she loved her.

"Did you know your friend was a lesbian, bi-sexual or whatever you want to call it?"

"No, I didn't," answered Kayra sadly.

"For the past six years, she has had several girlfriends. Most recently, she wrote of a sexual encounter with you, Ms. Austin!"

"What do you mean a sexual encounter?" shouted Kayra defensively. "I'm not like that! Pam was my best friend!"

"I think you're lying, Ms. Austin. I know this must be embarrassing for you. According to our research, it was a known fact that your friend was able to seduce almost anyone she wanted. You moved here to Chicago and you probably weren't aware of your friend's torrent affairs — with some very influential people, I might add. The list includes the Mayor's wife and Senator Morgan. That really scares us! Do you know who he is, Ms. Austin?"

"No, not really. I think I might have heard his name before."

"Ms. Austin, he is one of the most powerful men in Washington right now. It's possible he might even be running for the Presidency next election. His only problem is, he has had a very questionable personal life. The big boys on the "Hill" think he's too friendly with a lot of the wrong people. The word around is, your friend Ms. Johnson might have been trying to blackmail the Senator with their affair. We were even told she had proof about his involvement with the Mafia. Both of which would be devastating to his chances of becoming President. I hope you can see how dangerous this man could be to your friend Pam. I'll give you some important advice. Stay away from your friend! I strongly suggest that you not even talk to her if she calls you."

The other detective, Mr. Williams, who had been listening, interrupted.

"Enough of that. Back to your statement, Ms. Austin. On the day of January 26, 1996, is when Ms. Johnson wrote the two of you had a lesbian affair."

"I'm not gay!" shouted Kayra.

"Well, please allow me to read you a passage from her diary. Maybe it will refresh your memory.

"*I finally got my chance to caress Kayra's beautiful body and taste that juicy kitten of hers. I've been after it for a long, long time. Whoo, it felt so good! Kayra must have thought so too because she didn't want me to stop. And when she tasted me, it was as if her tongue couldn't get enough of being inside me. I almost had given up on this day ever happening until I got the good news she had decided to move here to Chicago.*

Then when Jake broke her heart, she fell right into my arms. Now the only thing left for me to do, is to permanently get his ass out of her life! He's been trying to convince her to give him another chance and I got a feeling at some point she might give in. I don't have much time. I got to work out the final plans to set him up and then I'll have Kayra all to myself."

Kayra stood up and grabbed her purse. "I don't want to hear anymore!" she yelled and walked toward the large black doors to exit the confined and musty room. "I'm through talking to you, if you have anything else to say to me, do it through my attorney."

"We just might have to do that -- unless we can find this Jake character and your friend Ms. Johnson. All we want to do is clear this whole thing up. We got a dead girl and a killer on the loose! And whether you like it or not, you were the last person with Ms. Johnson. For all we know, you could have been in on a plot to kill her."

"Look, I called you to report the murder."

"Yes, but somebody set up this guy Jake to take the fall, and you wouldn't be the first criminal to report their own crime," he said as Kayra stormed out the room.

Chapter 17

A week later, while Indigo was gone again, Jake decided to do a little snooping around on his own. Not about the murder, but about Indigo. "Since she's not around, I might as well check out things while she's gone." He went upstairs to the bedrooms and rambled through all the closets and drawers. On the top shelves of one of the closets, he found a stack of old photo albums. He quickly stretched and pulled them down. Then he flopped on the floor and began looking through them one by one.

Two hours later, he stopped for a moment.

"Damn, I wonder what time it is? I've been sitting here for a helluva long time. I don't want Indigo to come back and bust me." Slowly, he walked around the house and saw a huge brass clock hung on the wall. "Okay, it's 8:17p.m here. That means it's 7:17p.m. in Chicago. I believe I can catch Malik at home now and see if he has gotten any information for me. I know I probably don't want to hear whatever he has to say. Alright, where is the phone? I can't find shit in this damn house! There it is." Jake picked up the receiver and dialed Malik's number as quickly as he could.

"Hello."

"What's up, man? This is Jake!"

"Jake! Jake! Where are you man? Don't you know that cops are everywhere trying to find your ass. They've even been over here."

"They have?"

"Yes, they have."

"What did you tell them?"

"I didn't really tell them anything. I told them that I wasn't that close of a friend and I have no idea where you would be. Before you say anything else, I got to tell this. I was at the old Levi shop and talked to Papa Dee.

"Papa Dee is still around? His ass retired from the police department when they still had covered wagons and Indians and shit," said Jake with a smile.

"Yeah, but he still knows everything that goes down in the streets and in the police department. I don't know how he does it, but he knows. Anyway, he said the word on the street is, the woman who was killed was a friend of a girl named Pam. She is the same girl who was with your girl, Kayra at the club the night you got busted with Yolanda."

"That's where I recognized the name from!" said Jake.

"Apparently, they believe somebody was trying to kill Pam. Awhile back she accommodated some big Hollywood actor and his wife by having a mènage à trois, as a favor for him. The guy got pussy whipped and gave her a shit load of money. Pam didn't want to kick it with him nor his wife anymore and she ran off with the cash. The police think he paid somebody to kill her for revenge. Just so happen the night the killer came, Pam had another woman there with her and somehow they killed the wrong woman. Pam escaped. The only reason the police are still looking for you is to ask you some questions since you were the last person at the scene."

Jake dropped to his knees.

"Thank God! But why didn't you call and tell me?"

"I thought my phone might have been bugged. They would've caught me in a lie if I called you, since I had already told them I didn't know where you were. When are you going to tell Indigo what happened? I know she'll be glad to get rid of your ass!"

"Well, believe it or not, things have been alright between us. I sense they could get even better, if I had more time here. Adversity has a way of bringing people together."

"What are you saying Jake? You're not going to tell her that you're free to leave. You are a sick motherfu...." Malik stopped himself.

Jake tried to explain.

"I'm going to tell her. I don't want her to think that I'm a murderer. All I'm trying to say is, I want a little more time, maybe a couple of more days, to see what's up between us. Who knows when I might get a chance like this again to stay here with her and Railey like a real family."

"Look Negro, you're not a family anymore. Quit fooling yourself!" said Malik.

"You can say what you want to, Indigo and I will always be a part of each other's life. And Railey will always be a part of both our lives. To me, that makes us a family as far as I'm concerned. Just do me a favor. Go by my stores and make sure everything is okay. Check and make sure my people don't need anything. Tell them I'll be back next week, maybe Monday or Tuesday. Can you do that for me?"

Malik thought about what Jake said and agreed that he might not be sensitive enough to what he was going through as far as Indigo was concerned. "You know you're still my boy. I'll take care of it!"

"Thanks. I love you, man!"

"I love you too, my brother."

They hung up the phone and Jake yelled out again.

"Thank you God!" He jumped and tried to click his heels together, like one of the old Toyota commercials. "All I did was call to get some information and just like that, it's over!"

"Just like what?" asked Indigo.

Jake turned and saw Indigo standing in the hallway behind him. "Nothing." Jake quickly answered. "I was just thinking out loud."

"Hmmm, I bet you were. "You know that can be dangerous for you!" said Indigo laughing.

"Ha! Ha! " said Jake. He and Indigo talked for awhile and then decided they should turn in for the night. Jake still wanted to get a little touchy feely, but Indigo thought it would be best if they left that alone for now.

♥

The next morning Indigo heard a door open and saw a little head peeping around the corner of the bedroom door.

"Who's there?" asked Indigo softly.

"Oh hi, mom." answered Railey still half asleep.

"Hi, baby. You sure have been asleep a long time."

"I know, but I'm woke now. What are we doing today?"

"Well little man, it's Saturday, no school!"

"Where's daddy?"

"Here I am." shouted Jake from the guest bedroom. Go get one of your Nintendo games and I will play it with you for one hour. Now is that fair?" asked Jake.

"That's fair," replied Railey.

"Now that's settled, I went to the store early this morning and I need some help putting up these groceries," said Indigo as she casually walked out the room. She looked over her shoulder at Jake and gave him a flirtatious smile.

Jake and Railey put off their fun to give Indigo a hand. All they did was get in the way, but at least she was able to make them get off their butts, especially Jake. After all, the food she brought was really all for him. Indigo was very health conscious and carefully watched what she ate. It showed in her shapely body that was to die for.

Finally they were able to begin their game of *Earthworm Jim 2*, which Jake didn't have a clue how to play. Of course, Railey was more than happy to teach him. He kept making up his own rules to accommodate any errors he made, to keep whipping Jake into submission. After an hour of taking Railey's abuse, Jake convinced him to give it up for the morning and try again another time.

"That's it for me. You won!"

"Oh, daddy!" sighed Railey even though he was very pleased to have shown his daddy how good he could play.

"Don't, oh daddy me, we'll play again before I leave."

"I'm sure glad you're here with me and mommy. Are you going to stay with us now? I don't want you to go!"

Stunned by Railey's comment, Jake found himself trying his best to hold back the tears that had rolled up in his eyes. He didn't want to make any promises he wouldn't be able to keep. Who knows how things might turn out between him and Indigo. "Son, I really don't know how to answer that right now. Your mother and I are friends and always will be. Hopefully, one day we can work things out and we'll all be together again. But, no matter what, we'll always love you. Don't ever worry about that. I promise, I will always be a part of your life. I want to see you one day grow up to be a doctor, preacher, singer or whatever you want to be. I'll be right there shouting, hey, that's my son!"

Jake left and slowly closed Railey's door and went to find Indigo. She was seated in her all black and white living room, equipped with a large two-way marble fireplace, which faced her bedroom and den. She saw Jake standing in the doorway, quietly looking at her. She didn't know whether he was in deep thought or just felt too uncomfortable to say anything to her.

"Why don't you come in here and make yourself comfortable and quit standing there like a statue," invited Indigo as she made another try at starting the fireplace.

"Let me help you with that," insisted Jake. He walked to Indigo and gently pulled the poker out of her hand. Indigo smiled as Jake rearranged the kindling underneath the logs and lit them. Once he got the fire roaring, he looked at Indigo. He wanted to let her know that it could be useful having him around.

"There. Is that a good enough fire for you?" asked Jake standing up and handing Indigo the poker back.

"Yes it is, thanks," replied Indigo. She sat down on the floor on top of the white bear skin rug that laid in front of the fireplace. For some reason, she felt like some company and actually talking to Jake.

"Grab a seat," said Indigo.

"I'll be right back," replied Jake. He ran back to the closet and got the photo albums he saw before. He figured he would explain that he accidentally found them earlier while he was looking for something for Railey. He knew it sounded weak, but it would have to do as an explanation. Besides, Indigo would probably know he was just snooping around, regardless of what lie he told her. He went into the closet and got the albums. He tucked them under his arm and brought them into the living room with Indigo.

"What do you have now, Jake?"

"Just a little something I found earlier," said Jake as he took them from under his arm and showed Indigo what he had. "See, I found these!" Jake waved the albums in the air.

"Where did you get those from? I haven't seen those old pictures in a long time."

"I told you, I found them in one of your closets, while I was looking for something for Railey," insisted Jake. He really didn't sound too convincing, but he decided to stick by his story anyway.

"I see you're still a liar. Railey was asleep the whole time I was gone, so I know you weren't trying to find something for him. Your ass was just snooping around being nosey. Weren't you?"

Jake knew she was right and he didn't want to spoil the moment. He "fessed" up and admitted she was right.

"Okay, you got me. Anyway, I wanted to look at these with you."

"That's what I thought," said Indigo.

Jake walked to the fireplace and sat down next to Indigo. He opened the albums, which were filled with old pictures of him and her when they were married.

"Here, look at this one," said Jake. "It's a picture of you and me in Aruba for our honeymoon. We went snorkeling that day. I remember how scared you were. You held on to me so tight, I could hardly keep myself a float."

"Well, at least I tried it. Snorkeling was something I had wanted to do since I was a little girl."

"I think you told me about it on our first date together. I knew then, if we were ever to be together it would be one of the first things I would do for you," replied Jake.

"I still remember that day," smiled Indigo. "You promised me you were going to take me. It was the same day you took me to Corpus Christi for the weekend. We went on the beach late one Saturday night. You surprised me with a picnic on top of a big white blanket. It was complete with candles, a bottle of champagne and strawberries dipped in chocolate—which you fed to me one by one. You said how much you were in love with me and asked me to be your wife."

"I remember that night. It's like it was last night," replied Jake "We had been dating for a little while and were inseparable. We enjoyed each other's company so much that we never wanted to be apart. I had never met a woman like you, whom I had so much in common with and who, I could always open up to and be myself. I still remember all of the secrets we shared in those intimate conversations about the things going on in our lives. Then the hours we spent together making love. You were the only woman who I really felt had my back. I had to ask you to marry me. I loved you!"

"Is that right?"

135

"That's right!"

"Well Jake, that was the most romantic and special night of my life. From the moment you proposed, I knew I was in love. I mean really in love for the first time."

"Me too, Indigo. Me too. I believe it was the first time I really knew what love was."

Indigo turned to Jake and gently touched his chin with her finger.

"You know what they say don't you?"

"What?"

"It's never as good as the first time."

"Is that what *they* say?"

"That's what *they* say."

The two continued with their browsing of the photo albums. Jake pointed out a Christmas holiday picture of him and her putting up their Christmas tree.

"Do you remember that night?" asked Jake.

Indigo smiled and blushed. During that night when they were putting up the tree, she got horny watching Jake struggle with the large eight-foot tree. Indigo started seducing him by taking off all her clothes and wrapping herself in a roll of red ribbon.

"I remember alright," answered Indigo.

"I was trying my best to get that tree up and the lights put on, when you walked in with nothing on but the red ribbon! You stood in front of me feeling your breasts. And then you made me watch, as you entertained yourself until you almost came. I must have broken a record putting up those lights. I wrapped shit around that tree so fast, I almost started a fire."

Indigo rolled on the floor, crying laughing. She remembered how funny Jake looked that night, as he was rushing to get the tree up to her satisfaction, while she distracted him with her teasing. Somehow he was able to finish and he and Indigo got their grove on until Christmas morning came.

"I must admit, we had it going on that night!" conceded Indigo raising up from the floor laughing.

"We sure did! We could have it going on every night, if you would give me another chance and we start over."

Jake shot right for the jugular and hopefully straight to her heart. Indigo didn't know what to say or how to react. It didn't seem fair for her to have to deal with Jake being a fugitive from the law and staying in her house. Besides, God only knew what kind of trouble he might be in. And now, he was asking for another chance to permanently come back into her life.

"Jake, don't. Just don't do this right now. There's too much going on right now for me to even consider any possibility of there ever being a you and me again," said Indigo. "A lot of time has passed since we've been together. And time changes things."

"I know I made mistakes, Indigo. And as you can see, I still make them but you know that's not who I really am."

"But that is what you're about! You mean well, Jake. God knows that. But you're not capable of being in someone's life without hurting them. If you weren't a good man, I never would have married you even though I was pregnant. The same qualities you had then, I know you still have them. I'm just not sure if I want to put myself through all the shit that comes with being with you!"

Chapter 18

Kayra was now at a local restaurant after her ordeal at the precinct and had decided to have an early dinner. She needed a drink—a stiff one. She got the attention of the waiter and ordered the only drink she knew—rum and coke. He gladly took her request.

"I'll be right back with your drink and Ms., if you don't mind me saying, it looks like you could use it."

"It does huh? I just remembered something. Make that drink I ordered a cognac, room temperature with no ice. It reminds me of somebody I once knew," sighed Kayra. *"I just don't believe my damn life. Shit follows me, no matter where I go or who I see. Pam, how could you do this to me? I was in love with you. Hell, I contemplated changing my whole way of life just to be with you. Now, I find out she's involved in a murder and that I was nothing more than a piece of pussy to her. What kind of slut is that bitch to be doing this shit to people? I guess I don't know who Pam is anymore. She's not the woman I grew up with and was like sister to me."*

"Here you are. Enjoy and I hope things get better." said the waiter.

"Thank you and please don't go too far. I'll be ordering another one again real soon!"

"Okay," answered the waiter smiling.

"Bye," said Kayra dryly, taking a gulp of her drink. She choked and realized that maybe drinking might not be the way to deal with her problems. "Damn! This stuff is strong. Hmmm, but after the numbness goes away it taste pretty good," she mumbled while feeling the effects from the alcohol. "This better be my only one, or else somebody will have to carry me out of here."

Still buzzing from the cognac, Kayra wondered how she was going to find Pam and get to the bottom of all this. One part of her wanted Pam to suffer for what she had done. But she knew in her heart, letting go wouldn't be that easy. Plus, if she didn't find Pam the police would probably think she had somehow conspired with Pam to set up Jake.

Chapter 19

*J*ake and Indigo continued to reminisce about the love they once shared.

"Would it make a difference if all this about the murder wasn't going on?" asked Jake as he considered telling her the truth instead of waiting until after the weekend.

"Of course it would make a difference. Either way, it still wouldn't be an automatic yes, I'll get back with you! I make no secret about it, I still love you. Also, on an occasion or two we've gotten our freak on. Hey, I make no apologies for still enjoying being single. In fact, I love being a single black woman! Indigo looked around her house with her arms opened. "As you can see, I do a pretty damn good job at taking care of myself and our son. I really don't need a man in my life to do anything for me, except to give me a little bit when I want it! I know that might sound like whatever, but that's just the way it is. I got my freedom and I take good care of our son. I provide him with a good life.

What more can you offer me, Jake? Tell me. What more can you offer me but more headaches? I already got them from you being here just a few days!"

"I don't know what else to say. You got me all fucked up! If it makes you feel any better, I'm cleared of the murder!"

"What do you mean?"

"I called Malik while you were gone. He got information from a friend of ours, who has connections in the police department. He said that the killer was trying to kill a friend of Kayra's named Pam. It's somebody who she used to be involved with, who's trying to kill her—not me. There you have it. I'm not part of all that shit anymore."

"Why didn't you tell me this when I first walked in? Why did you wait half the damn night before you said anything?"

"You want the truth? Do you?" asked Jake.

"Yes, I want the truth!" answered Indigo loudly.

"I wasn't going to tell you at all. At least, not right now. I wanted to wait and tell you after the weekend. I wanted to have more time to spend with you and Railey. But now since we've had our little talk, I see no reason to do that now. There, you have all of the truth! Do you feel better?"

"I don't know how I feel. I'm glad you won't be going to jail. That means Railey and I aren't in any more danger. As far as anything else, it's just going to take time. If you want to stay here a little while longer, you can. It will give you more time with Railey," suggested Indigo.

"You're right. From talking to him tonight, he really wants me around. I'll stay until the weekend is over. Maybe I'll send for Railey in a couple of months when he gets a break from school."

"That's fine. Look, I don't want you to be upset or hurt by what I said. You are my first love and the father of my beautiful child. I know you like no other, just give me some time."

"I'm going for a walk. Do you want me to put out the fire before I leave?" asked Jake.

"No, it's already gone," answered Indigo quietly, referring to the flame in her heart.

Chapter 20

"I know what I'm going to do. I'll go home and simply wait. If I have any chance at all of finding her, it will be only if she contacts me. Hopefully, everything wasn't a complete lie and she has enough feelings for me to let me know she's alright. Maybe, she will even apologize for all the shit she put me through." Kayra signaled for the waiter to come over to her table.

"Yes, is it time for another drink?"

"No, I decided it's best if I just go home and work things out."

"Very well, I think that's a wise choice. Here's your check. I look forward to serving you again soon."

Kayra quickly gave the waiter a twenty-dollar bill and told him to keep the change. She raced out of the restaurant and hurried home. When she got there, the first thing she saw was her answering machine flashing with a message. "I wonder who that is. I know it's not Pam calling already, or is it?" She slowly walked to the green flashing light, which seemed to blink faster in sequence with her racing heartbeat. "Let's see." Kayra pushed the button and heard noises in the background before an abrupt hang up. "That's strange! I wonder who that was. Well, I'll be here the next time it rings. I know she's going to call—I just know it! When she does, all I want to know is why she lied to me? Did all she want to do was fuck me? I'd be a fool to think Pam is going to suddenly change her ways just for me. There must be a motive for her doing all this shit. There's got to be. Is it for the money? She has a legitimate and successful business here in Chicago. Pam would not have given that up just to get in my panties! Would she? That's what I have to find out!"

Chapter 21

*J*ake and Indigo didn't say very much to each other over the weekend. Jake was still greatly disappointed that things didn't turn out like he had hoped.

Indigo observed how much Railey missed Jake, and she enjoyed seeing him so happy. Railey enjoyed his weekend with his dad and Jake loved spending quality time with him instead of doing his usual long-distance parenting. It was pleasing to know Railey still insisted on a real relationship with his dad. He was not willing to settle for the temporary attention given to him by the few men Indigo would have over for an occasional date. She didn't do much of that, partly because of her busy schedule, but mainly because she really wasn't interested in having a steady man in her life. Therefore, Railey's only interaction with a male figure was mostly limited to the times that Jake would fly out or send for him on holiday weekends.

That concerned Indigo. The last thing she wanted was a son who had a little *sugar in his blood*. She had an uncle in the family who was sweet. All she ever heard when they got mad at him was, "that faggot this or that faggot that!" Indigo was determined nobody was ever going to call her baby a faggot—at least, not if she could help it!

♥

When Monday morning came, Railey and Indigo took Jake to the airport. Jake insisted that they not come inside with him. He didn't want to make a big teary-eyed scene, which almost was about to happen anyway, just as they pulled up to the check-in counter. Indigo parked in the Northwest curbside check-in station. The skycap took Jake's suitcase from the trunk. Jake, Railey and Indigo all hugged as the tears rolled down their faces. Afterwards, Jake quietly picked Railey up and gave him one last big hug and kiss.

"You do good in school and take care of your mother. I love you very much. Call me next week and tell me how everything is going with school."

"Okay, daddy. I love you, too!"

"I'm sorry for all the trouble. I wish things had turned out differently—I tried." apologized Jake.

"Jake, it was no trouble at all. I think Railey benefited from all this. Besides, it was kinda exciting having a real live fugitive hide-a-way in my house. As far as you and me, I wish things could have been different too. Who knows what the future holds. Hang in there and stay your butt out of trouble for a change. Most of all, leave those women alone! Come here." Indigo grabbed Jake's shirt and pulled him closer to her.

"What do you want?" Jake whispered.

"Just come here," replied Indigo again.

Jake moved closer and Indigo whispered in his ear. She grabbed a hand full of his manhood and gently squeezed. "Keep this in your pants. Give yourself some time to think with your little head up there, instead of this big one down here!" she laughed. "Trust me, I've

150

been praying for us. I know God will let me know, if and when the time is right for you and me again."

Indigo slowly let go of her grip and gave Jake a big kiss on the cheek.

"Bye," laughed Indigo as she and Jake giggled at what she had just done.

"Bye to you, too, and thanks! Bye, Railey."

Indigo and Railey got back in the car and drove off. Jake watched and tried to keep from shedding another tear. He tipped the skycap and went inside to the terminal for his flight.

♥

Malik picked Jake up at the airport and took him home a free man. There was still some unfinished business to take care of with the police, although it was nothing compared to when he left.

After giving his statement to the police, Jake was released and was free to go as he pleased. In fact, they apologized for all the troubled they caused him. It was a total reversal of script from the way the police normally dealt with a black man, which came as a pleasant surprise.

The only thing left for Jake to do now was to go to church with Malik like he had promised him weeks ago. After everything, now seemed like the perfect time to go. Jake wasn't much of a Christian man, but surely God had been more than kind to him for getting him out of the big mess he had been in. Like all southern mamas, Jake's mother always told him to remember to "give thanks to God for all he's done for you." Certainly, he had done a lot for Jake throughout his life, with little in return from him. Jake vowed to change all that now. Before Malik left, he made Jake promise no matter what, he would go to church on Sunday. Malik agreed. "It's about time!" he said.

As soon as Malik got home, he called Pastor Wilson to let him know they would be coming for service Sunday. He was so happy to hear from Malik, he invited both him and Jake to have dinner at his house after the evening service. Of course, Malik gladly accepted and called Jake to ask him if he had any problems with going. Jake thought it was a good idea. He had some questions he wanted to ask, plus he wanted to get some spiritual counseling, which he felt he needed badly!

Chapter 22

After waiting all evening and half the night for Pam to call, Kayra eased herself to bed. It had been a trying day listening to the two asshole detectives tell her Pam was just using her for sex. Like a onetime mistake with Pam made her a lesbian and a slut. *"What gives them the right to judge me and say who I can and cannot sleep with. I'm a grown woman and if I'm attracted to somebody, whether it's a woman or whoever, it's my choice! I shouldn't have to be labeled. I wonder who they fuck at night when they leave their little police world!"*

Kayra finally dozed off to sleep. When she woke up it was two o'clock in the morning and there was still no word from Pam as Kayra napped on and off. By now, she knew it was unlikely Pam would be calling. She made herself comfortable by taking off her clothes and putting on a set of silk pajamas. She pulled back the covers and thought how nice it would feel to climb into bed and get some real sleep, instead of waking up at every sound she heard. "It's two o'clock, hopefully she will call tomorrow or should I say, later today."

She fell back on the bed and pulled the warm covers over her chilled body. Then the phone rang.

"Damn! Who is this? I was just about to go to sleep." Kayra grabbed the phone angrily and put it to her ear. "What! Who is this? Don't you know what time it is?"

"I know what time it is, but is that any way to talk to an old friend?" said the voice quietly on the other end.

"Pam, is that you?" asked Kayra throwing the covers off her body and sitting up.

"Yes, it's me. Don't say anything yet. First, is anybody there with you now?"

"No," answered Kayra too frightened to talk.

"Good. Has anybody suspicious been there asking about me?"

"No! Now, what's this all about Pam? I got the police coming up to the school and taking me to the station. They asked me a bunch of questions that I didn't have the answers to. Most of all, I thought you were dead. The night all this happened, Jake came in your house and when I saw him bending over that body, I thought it was you!"

"Calm down Kayra. I know I have a lot of explaining to do. First, look out your window very carefully and tell me whether you see a car."

"Look Pam! I'm not going to play "peeping tom" for you. It's nobody out there. If you got problems, you need to take care of them. Leave me out of it! I'm not going to be a part of this murder, lying and stealing. It's too much for me to deal with. It's just too much, you hear me!" screamed Kayra. She was about to hang up the phone before Pam stopped her and tried to explain.

"Kayra, listen to me."

"No! I'm not listening to you anymore. I tried listening to you when you told me you loved me. I tried listening to you when you told me I was the only woman you've been with. I'm tired of listening to you.

You're no better than Jake and all the rest!" yelled Kayra crying into the pillow on her bed.

"Kayra, I didn't have anything to do with Dee Dee getting killed. I admit, I did lie about not being with another woman. I thought if I told you the truth, you would think I was some kind of freak or something. I was intimate with Dee Dee that night. She is or was a very close friend of mine. I met her when I first moved to Chicago and things just kinda happened between us. That night, all I remember is Dee Dee getting up to take a bath before she left to go home. I was in the guest bedroom looking for a robe to put on. Then I heard the back window break and people storming inside the house. I was scared to death and hid in the closet until they left. I got up and went into the bedroom to check on Dee Dee. That's when I found her in the bathroom dead! I didn't know what else to do. I got the hell out of there before they realized they had killed the wrong person and came back looking for me. I ran out the back door and drove until I found a place to hide. Then I called the police."

"Yeah, but what about the money you stole and all the other scandalous shit you did? That's why you got somebody trying to kill you in the first place! The police said it was because of an affair you had with an actor and his wife. You screwed both of them and then ran off with their money. They also told me about some big whiz Senator you were messing around with. He's supposed to run for President. Now he's afraid that you have some stuff about his past that will ruin him!

"They told you that?" asked Pam terrified to hear the answer.

"Yes. Hell, they even warned me he might be the one trying to have you killed and warned me I should stay as far away from you as possible. I don't know who you are anymore, Pam. The bad part is that I fell in love with you. Of all things, I fell in love with you. A woman. My friend. You see what you do to people's lives!"

Chapter 23

At church on Sunday morning, Pastor Wilson was in the middle of the visitor's welcome just as Malik and Jake walk through the doors. Both of them looked up to see if there were any signs of lightning striking. It had been a long absence and years of sinning and grinning. Pastor Wilson spotted them entering. He signaled the ushers to include them in the passing of the microphone for visitors to acknowledge the congregation. Malik and Jake listened to the other visitors say their greetings, which all sounded the same.

"Giving thanks to God. Amen. For allowing me to be here this morning. Amen. I would like to say good morning to Pastor Wilson, Deacons, Ushers, Amen, and to the congregation, Amen. I thank God for waking me up this morning because he didn't have to do it, Amen."

"Amen sister!" shouted a woman nearby.

"Thank you Jesus for allowing me to worship you and to praise your Holy name, Amen. Thank you, Amen. I'll look forward to visiting here again real soon."

"Thank you for those loving words," continued Pastor Wilson. His attention now turned to Jake and Malik.

"Would you two young brothers who just walked in like to say a few words to the congregation?"

Each declined gracefully, by shaking their heads "no."

"Well, may God bless you anyway," said Pastor Wilson smiling at Malik.

The usher showed Malik and Jake to the only available seats, which were in the *Hallelujah* section. All the women had on big hats and held paper fans they received from ushers at the entrance of the church—— of course, it wasn't even hot. The building was completely air conditioned, but the *Hallelujah* section still couldn't stop vigorously fanning themselves as they rocked back and forth.

"As pastor of Holiday Baptist Church, I would like to thank all of the visitors for coming and sharing God's word with us today. I sincerely hope this will not be your last time worshipping with us. May God bless you and keep you. The choir will come and bring you a couple of selections before we get started with our lesson for the day. Thank you."

The choir stood up and sang two wonderful songs that had the *Hallelujah* section up on their feet praising the Lord and jumping for joy. Jake was even moved by one of the selections.

Afterwards, Pastor Wilson got up and began his sermon.

"Turn in your Bible to the...." Before Jake and Malik knew it, they found themselves in the middle of five large women who had gotten up and started the *Holy Ghost* dance, jumping and throwing their hands in the air. One of the women even accidentally elbowed Jake in the eye.

"Damn!" he mumbled before he realized what he said.

"What did you say?" asked Malik surprised at what he thought he heard Jake say.

"Man, she hit me in the eye!" whispered Jake.

"You can't be cursing in here. Have you been listening to anything the Pastor been preaching about for the last half-hour?" asked Malik.

"Well, not really, with the "sho-nuf" sisters jumping around! It's hard for me to pay attention to anything. I'm sorry."

"Don't worry, it'll be over with soon."

"I hope so!" said Jake anxiously.

Chapter 24

Kayra sat and waited for Pam. She thought she had just made the biggest mistake of her life by letting Pam come over. But she had to see her one more time to make Pam look her in her eyes and tell her she hadn't meant for this to happen. Thirty minutes passed and Kayra rose out of her chair as she heard a car pulling in the driveway.

"That must be her," said Kayra looking out the window. She didn't recognize the small black car and tried to see if Pam was inside. Suddenly, Kayra heard a tap on the door and ran to look through the tiny peephole. All she saw was a scarf tied around a bended down head.

"Pam. Is that you?" whispered Kayra through the door.

"Yes," a low muffled voice answered.

Kayra quickly opened the door and let out a big smile.

The sound of three shots quickly rang through the air, hitting Kayra in the head once and twice in the

162

chest. The force from the large caliber gun threw Kayra onto the floor, giving her only one glance at her murderer.

"We meet again, Ms. Austin. I warned you at the station to stay away from your friend, but you didn't listen."

The detective turned as he heard a door close. It was Pam. She had parked around the block and walked through the alley behind Kayra's house. She came through the back door and used the key Kayra had given her a few months ago. When she entered the room, she saw Kayra lying on the floor.

"Kayra!" she shouted without seeing the detective standing behind the door.

"Ms. Johnson," shouted the detective as Pam jumped and turned around.

"This is from the Senator, not your Hollywood friend. I'm afraid his people got a little delayed."

After the shots, Pam's body dropped and rested on top of Kayra's.

Chapter 25

"*D*inner was good. Your wife got it going on!" said Jake smiling as he patted his stomach.

"I know. Why do you think I married her!" laughed Pastor Wilson. But Jake, Malik tells me you might want a little spiritual advice and guidance."

Jake looked sharply at Malik like, *no you didn't* and then acknowledged the Pastor's comment. "Yes sir, I do."

"What exactly is your concern Jake?"

"It's me and women. I just can't seem to be committed to one. No matter how much in love I am, I end up fu...I mean messing it up. Usually, because I try to screw other women. Sorry, but that's just the way it's been. And the other thing, I wanted to talk about was God. My mother brought me up in the church. I can even remember getting baptized and being what you call 'saved'. But now I don't feel the same about it anymore."

"What do you mean Jake?" asked the Pastor.

165

"I have done a lot of stuff, and God only knows the last time I was at a church before today. I remember my mother saying back then, 'once you're saved, you're always saved.' But I just don't feel like a Christian or saved or whatever you want to call it, anymore."

"Do you still believe?"

"You mean in God and Jesus? Yes, I do!"

"I think I understand now. Let me tell you a real quick story about myself that I believe will help you. Back in the days before I was a Preacher, they used to call me 'Chill Will.' I ran the streets and women with the best of them. One day I stopped and asked myself, "was this what I wanted to do with the rest of my life?" Back in those days it seemed like I could never be satisfied. The more women I would, like you say 'screw', the more I wanted.   Even drugs. The more weed I smoked, the more I wanted. I just couldn't get enough. After a while, it wears you down. Then one Sunday morning I got up and decided I was going to church with one of my women friends at the time. She's the same woman who fixed dinner for us and who I now call my wife. In church that day, hearing the sermon quenched my spirit more than anything I had ever tried before. It satisfied me more than the drugs and more than the women. From that day on, I've been constantly seeking the Lord. So you can do it too, son! All you got to is *draw nigh unto him and he'll draw nigh unto you.* Believe me, God is more than able to help you overcome whatever you're going through, as a man or as a Christian. As far as being saved. Do you know what that means?"

"No, not really."

"To be saved means you have accepted Jesus Christ to be your Lord and Savior. You believe God loved you so much *he* sent his only son to Earth to die on the cross for your sins and he resurrected. He did it so if you are saved, you repent and ask God to forgive you when you sin. He will! That's it in a nutshell. The rest is about lifestyle choices and being faithful, which is to be like Jesus Christ. He's your role model. In order to be like him, guess what? You've got to grow like a baby grows, one step at a time. Reading your Bible, praying the word and then going to Church to hear the word."

After Jake and Malik finished listening to Pastor Wilson, he walked them to the door and they all said good night. "Are you two coming back to Church and visit us again?"

"I am," answered Malik first, and then he looked at Jake.

"Yes, I'll be there too!"

"Great!" replied Pastor Wilson happily.

"One thing though," asked Jake.

"What's that?" asked the Pastor.

"Can we not sit in the *'Hallelujah'* section yet. I got to grow into that!"

"Get there earlier next time." laughed Pastor Wilson.

♥

Jake went home as quickly as he could after dropping Malik off. As he settled in for the night, he kept thinking about Pastor Wilson's impromptu sermon that he had given him at his house. Then the phone rang and startled Jake.

"I wonder who this is? Hello."

"Hi, Jake, this is Yolanda. Where have you been? I've been trying to find you the past few days."

"I've been with a good friend of mine."

"I miss you. Can I come over there? I've gotten horny thinking about you today."

Jake looked down at his penis, which was starting to grow at the thought of Yolanda's fine body being next to him — even though he really didn't feel like being bothered with her. Just as he was going to tell her yes, he stopped. "No, not tonight Yolanda. As a matter fact, not any night. I don't mean to be rude, but I don't think it's a good idea for us to see each other anymore."

"But Jake, what are you talking about? Why are you doing this?" asked Yolanda desperately.

"It's time for a change! Bye Yolanda." Jake hung up the phone. He felt good about controlling his desires.

~~Chapter~~ 26

*S*pring finally came to the "Windy City" and was starting to thaw out all the winter snow. It had been four months and the police still hadn't found out who killed Kayra. Her death and the circumstances surrounding that night, was as the police classified it "inconclusive."

Jake sat and glanced out the window. *"What a winter this has been,* he thought. *I couldn't have asked for more excitement. I fell in love–God rest her soul; got accused of murder; watched Malik, who up to a few months ago couldn't buy a woman, get married. I do wish the best for him and Nicole; I even got a chance to move back with Indigo and Railey–too bad it was only temporary. All this sounds like a good plot for a novel. Anyway, the main thing is I finally got saved! Or better said, I reaffirmed my relationship with God because I never stopped being saved."*

Jake took a break from his Bible studying to go to the kitchen to get a glass of juice when the phone suddenly rang. He answered and to his surprise, it was Indigo.

"Hi, Jake. How are you?"

"Fine Indigo, I'm just fine. This is certainly a surprise."

"Well, it shouldn't be. Don't you remember me telling you all you have to do is give me some time and God would let me know what I should do about you and me."

"Yes, I remember that. What are you going to do?" asked Jake anxiously.

"You mean, what are *we* going to do? Let's make it better than the first time!" answered Indigo.

EXCERTS FROM THE UPCOMMING RELEASE

BUTT NAKED,
MY SOUL EXPOSED!

Naked 1

It was love gone full circle. One man. One woman. One child. Most of all, one love. Who would've thought in less than three years, things would get so dangerous and out of control. It's not like Indigo and I didn't already have our share of problems with trying to make our reincarnated relationship work. And what made the whole ordeal even more frightening was the danger it has put our son Railey in. To jeopardize his life was the end of the rope for me. I swear, if something had happened to him I would have killed that bitch Pam! She was responsible for getting me and my family wrapped-up-in, of all things...murder. This was all her damn fault! What started out as just a daring affair, soon turned into a terrible nightmare that just wouldn't go away.

In the center of it all, was my black ass. And why? I'll tell you why. An innocent attraction to a beautiful schoolteacher named, Kayra Austin. She was an angel unaware of her fate with a short-lived life full of fallen loves, which began long before I came into her life. Unfortunately, at the time we met and started our yearlong relationship, I was still not the man I wanted to be.

Before we knew what happened both of us fell hook line and sinker in love or whatever it was we were in. I'll stick to love; at least that's how we felt at the time and shit, who can tell the difference. At any rate, it became evident; I would suffer for my transgressions for whatever damage I stood accused of inflicting to her already fragile heart.

Friday began like most had several times before. We laid quiet and still. Our nude bodies frozen. Pacified by a night of strong, wild and free lovemaking. The sheets underneath us still wet from the sweat of the intenseness we shared. Neither one of us could believe in less than a week we would be jumping the broom for the second time around. Today would be our last "date day" before we became man and wife again.

Therefore, the excitement built inside us like a raging river eager to explode into the sea. Explode, we did! In, around and on each other. Charge it to the strong love we shared. The burning passion inside us. The busy schedules that monopolized our time and kept us from frequently seeing each other. Or the fact, we weren't living together yet. A decision we made together to avoid getting too comfortable with our renewed relationship too soon. It helped us maintain freshness, while we took our time getting to know one another again. Each time we were together felt like our very first time.

When Indigo and I finally regained consciousness and aroused from our bliss, I gently kissed her about the neck to wake her. The affection was returned and I felt the touch of her moist lips pressed again mine. I accepted the unspoken invitation to take my kiss further down her smooth honey brown body. A choice encouraged by the hand I felt firmly guiding my head. Before long, we found ourselves intertwined once again.

Afterwards, Indigo escorted me to the large bathroom, located some fifty feet from the canopy bed across the huge master suite. The round Roman tub filled with hot suds, while we discussed the final arrangements of the wedding next week. We concluded we had too many things left to do for us to lay around making love all day. Not! The tub was now full near capacity and the next hour was filled with slow playful lovemaking and quick bathing.

Later, we decided to do brunch at the Hotel Hilton and take a walk along Coney Island. By day's end we were back home spending the remainder of the evening making calls and filling out invitations. The nightfall came before we knew it and by 9:oopm we had completed what seemed like a week's worth of work. But who's complaining. I was thankful all our friends and family would be in Chicago to show their love and give us much needed support. This reunion had been a long time coming for Indigo and I. These past few years had been difficult at best to deal with. Mainly, because the trust in our relationship had fleeted as quickly as it came when we first set eyes on one another back in '84.

I spent the rest of the night tossing with thoughts of what I could've and should've done much differently. How I could have sustained the love and the trust. For without trust, love is difficult to exist. Therefore, I choose to spend the rest of my life making Jake Alexander the best man he can possibly be. By doing so, I am blessed to be within a week of having my faithfulness rewarded.

With that comfort, we closed our eyes free of worry or concern. In fact, the peacefulness felt so good, we found ourselves not wanting to spoil it. We just laid there tangled together, nakedness over nakedness.

Through the years of pain, trials and joy, we shared the kind of love that only two people truly meant to be together could share. The solitude of the night engulfed us like cupped hands holding a fragile butterfly.

When we awoke the next morning, the phone rang off the hook from the second we got up. Everyone in Chicago called to make sure everything was still on.

Charlotte's call came around 10:30am to confirm our flight information. She had been the organizer of

Indigo's bachelorette party and all the wedding arrangements. In fact, it was her suggestion to celebrate in Chicago.

WELCOME TO

THE
POET'S
CORNER

WHERE THE SPOKEN WORD LIVES

The Studio presents The Poet's Corner where
Poets come to share their interpretations with
other artist and enthusiasts of the spoken word.

Note: Please enjoy my interpretations. However, due
to press deadline other poets could not be showcased
in this printing. Look for them in future printings or on
The Studio's official website.

I Wait. Almost.
poet: jonathan michael hicks

I wait.
Meditating on the thoughts that have long taken me by gentle breeze.
Almost.
Eased to the edge.
Deserted by the gentle breeze and now pushed by the storm of your voice.
I wait.
You call.
The whispers engage me.
Twine thigh asphyxiate me.
Surrendered arms have taken me.
The melted womb drenched to feel me.
Almost.
The gentle comes.
The storm goes.
It returns now built with flames from you lips placed on my shivering body.
I respond with buckled knees and a swollen flesh at the mere mention of your name.
Or thoughts about your melted essence.
I wait.
Now harden by the plates of your tongue.
Inspired by its vibrations.
Crazied 'til I can't stand.
Baptized by your body's fluids.
Led by the Holy Spirit of desire and resurrected by your love.
Almost.
The storms comes.
Gentle stays.
They meet.
Almost.
I wait.

The Essence of A Woman (remix)
poet: jonathan michael hicks

The essence of a woman inspired me today
I didn't know what to say
Never felt this way
I wanted to scream stay
Knew she wouldn't respond that way
I understood how to play
Our eyes met and soon *that* woman was my lady

That's Crazy
poet: jonathan Michael hicks

That's crazy for me to pace the wood
When it's late at night and I'm confused if I should
Beg you to stay or make you go for good
I would if I could
Stay positive on the mental assemblies, God please

That's crazy when everyone else can't understand what I felt
Through your butter embrace, my apprehensions melt
When I see your eyes they say something else
My own questions try to help
Like does she love me? Desire me? Is she being honest with me?
Or is there a history of infidelities
Stay positive on the mental assemblies, God please

That's crazy for all my thoughts to be you freakin' me
I want our love to be more than sexuality
But damn we can't ignore how good it is
It's just a reality, how you handle thee
I need your mouth on me
It's time we....
Stay positive on the mental assemblies, God please

That's crazy for us to hate so bad, and love so good
Happiness I should
Without all the bullshit you pull, maybe I would
I want you cooperation, not your attitude or frustrations
And I won't mention the sexual hesitations
Can't quit understand these pussy game demonstrations
Stay positive on the mental assemblies, God please

Let's talk about the possibilities
I'll wait and see if you're the one for me
Don't trip, it could be just my insecurities
Stay positive on mental assemblies, God please

That's crazy if you won't turn the page on this mess
Talkin' about you putting me to the test
Girl, you'll get put to the test
Somebody else be in your nest
Realize *I* was your pleasantness, if not....
God please, may he help you stay positive on the mental assemblies

Your Smile
poet: jonathan michael hicks

I love your big beautiful smile
You have a smooth, sexy laid-back style
Bet you can be fun and wild
But then again it's back to your smile

If I wrote for you
Flew for you
Cherished you
Would there be a problem being with you
Promise to never to say we're through
Let me see that smile boo